A Gift of Ice

Book Two of the
JIMMY FINCHER SAGA

A Gift of Ice

BY JAMES DASHNER

BONNEVILLE BOOKS
Springville, Utah

ISBN: 1-55517-753-0
e. 2

Published by Bonneville Books,
an imprint of Cedar Fort, Inc.
925 N. Main, Springville, Utah, 84663
www.cedarfort.com

Distributed by:

Cover design by Nicole Williams
Cover design © 2004 by Lyle Mortimer

Printed in the United States of America
10 9 8 7 6 5 4 3 2

Printed on acid-free paper

This one is for Lynette,
my reason for living.

OTHER BOOKS BY JAMES DASHNER

A Door in the Woods

BOOK ONE OF THE JIMMY FINCHER SAGA

The Tower of Air

BOOK THREE OF THE JIMMY FINCHER SAGA

War of the Black Curtain

BOOK FOUR OF THE JIMMY FINCHER SAGA

✧Acknowledgments✧

Once again, a lot of people helped this project come together. Thanks to all the people at Cedar Fort for being so great during this whole process. A huge thanks to Shirley Bahlmann for her unbelievable editing skills and advice. Thanks to Lewis Christian for "The Idea." And to everyone else who contributed, please know that I really appreciate you.

To the kids at R.E. Davis Elementary School in Sumter, South Carolina, thank you for reminding me of how magical reading books can be.

And more than anything, I want to thank my readers. It means so much to hear from you and know that you are enjoying this story. Happy reading.

✧Table of Contents✧

✧PROLOGUE✧

There are frightening things in Japan.

It seems like such a wonderful, exotic place. Majestic, ice-capped mountains and emerald forests, ancient temples and shrines, rushing rivers and breath-taking waterfalls. To a normal person, the lands of Japan would be the perfect setting for a vacation. But to me, the world was no longer normal.

My name is Jimmy Fincher, and mine is a story of wonder and dread. (And I really, really hate cooked peas, but that has nothing to do with this story.)

Only fourteen years old, I'd been set on a course that could not stop, or the world I called my own, along with countless others, would be in terrible jeopardy. The things I'd been through and the circumstances that led to my urgent arrival in the beautiful lands of Japan are difficult to summarize without sounding like a shoeless wacko from the backwoods of Georgia.

A conspiracy of crazed men, who were actually beings from another, darker place, trying to open a magical door. My dad, caught in the middle, doing his best to prevent them. Me, just a boy, the one destined to open it. A special gift received, one that made me indestructible.

The Givers, a mysterious people determined to help save our world from an enemy unprecedented in ruthlessness. The Black Curtain, that strange, unpredictable portal that led to The Blackness, a pathway between countless worlds. A new friend, Joseph, kidnapped by shadows with wings.

Permeating it all, a phrase that had grown to haunt us in our dreams.

The Stompers are coming.

This was the substance of my new life, and although it was more exciting than the old one, I wasn't particularly enjoying it.

In the days leading up to our arrival in Japan, unthinkable, unimaginable things had occurred. Our lives had been tossed and turned, pulled inside out, twisted, trampled upon. Everything was different now, we knew that, and had tried to fully accept it. Our perceptions on life had taken a turn at the crossroads.

My blocking of the Black Curtain was only days past. However, fear seemed to hover just around the corner. The questions lingered. Was the Curtain really sealed against the terrors of the Blackness? Were we safe from the Shadow Ka? Did we have enough time to find the Givers' book before the Stompers appeared, ready to wreak havoc? Where and how would we find the book, and what exactly was the Second Gift?

The questions went on and on.

In the wet, humid lands of Japan, some of these questions would be answered, and others would be born.

Dad had found us a nice little hotel in the middle of a city called Kushiro, one of the most fascinating places I'd ever visited—in this world, anyway. It was a town by the ocean, a place for fishing and huge shipping boats. My older brother Rusty and I were in constant awe at this different culture we had invaded. After entering the Blackness, we thought everything in our own world would be dull and ordinary. We were very wrong.

Japan was like discovering a new and thrilling book.

The streets were constantly packed with people, all

of them in a hurry to get somewhere. The buildings towered over us no matter where we went, and bright neon signs shone from every direction. The days and nights were misty and rainy, the streets soaked and slippery. The chattering of the Japanese language filled our ears, and it was like magic that people could actually understand each other. Old ladies shuffled through the streets in fancy robes called kimonos, and old men bowed to me without fail. Smells of fish and salt pounded our noses, and eerie music blasted from speakers up and down the streets. Japanese kids pointed at us, giggling, saying hello with really bad accents.

It was flat-out a different place. Sometimes I felt certain we had all been hit in the head during those last catastrophic moments in the Blackness, and that we had actually gone through another portal and were in some other, strange world. But no, this was just Japan, just another country in our world, now under threat from an unseen and unknown enemy. Just another country that I was supposed to save from the Stompers.

Of course, we all really wished we knew what a Stomper *was*.

At the hotel, we slept on the ground in rooms where the floor was made out of woven straw. The walls were paper-thin, and some old grandma kept coming into our rooms without asking and offering us herbal tea and weird-looking crackers. The telephone in our room wouldn't work unless you put coins in it. There was no shower, only a tub, and to go potty you had to do a magical balancing act over a hole in the bathroom floor. That was the toilet—forget sitting down.

Japan sometimes made the Blackness seem like a trip to the mall. Well, not really.

Our first few days in Japan were relaxed and easy, and we spent a lot of time exploring that strange and exotic place. Dad kept busy at an old library, looking at maps and recreating his adventures of the last time he'd been here. He said we'd be ready to start our search for the book pretty soon, and so my mom, Rusty, and I did a lot of waiting, and walking around, and eating weird food.

It's strange how things work out sometimes. My dad, the only one who had actually seen this book we sought, would never see it again, and would never take us to where it rested. In the weeks ahead, nothing, absolutely nothing, would go according to plan. So, really, those first few days were a complete waste.

All in all, however, it was a fun week. But, typical of the last month or two, things were about to take a turn for the worst.

Like I told you, mine is a tale of wonder and dread.

This is the story of Jimmy Fincher.

✧ ☽ ✧ ☽ ✧

The deafening roar that started my family's latest and greatest nightmare occurred during our seventh night in Japan.

It came from a new and unexpected enemy.

It came from the Bosu Zoku.

✧Chapter 1✧

The New Terror

The seventh day had been a really fun one, mostly spent walking up and down the beach, buying food from vendors while taking in the salty scent of the ocean. We spoke about the good old days before we discovered Raspy and Shadow Ka and little things like the fact that other worlds existed through black rips in the air called the Black Curtain.

By the time we returned to the hotel that night and had supper with Dad, we were exhausted from all of the walking. Dad too was tired from having looked at books and maps all day, and writing down his plans for us to find the mysterious book of the Givers that was going to solve all of our problems. We were in our hotel room by nightfall, and it was time to go to sleep—on the floor, of course.

"Dad," I asked as he and I were brushing our teeth in the bathroom, "what have you been thinking of the last few days?"

"What do you mean?" he replied.

"You know, about the Blackness and the book and all this stuff. I mean, we are in Japan, on a mission to find some mysterious book from another world. Don't you think it's kind of weird that we're all acting so normal, like we're just here on vacation or something?"

"Yeah, I guess so. But, if you think about it," Dad spread his hands and spoke through a thick foam of toothpaste, "What're we supposed to do?" He spat in the sink. "Should we sit in a corner and huddle together like a Shadow Ka will attack us at any minute? If I've learned anything in life, it's that you adapt quickly to your circumstances, and you can surprise yourself at how you just end up acting like everything is normal. We forget that the whole world is completely different than it used to be. For example . . ."

Dad grabbed one of the hotel cups, reached down to the sink and filled it with water, looked at it for a second, then heaved the water straight at my head. I flinched, ready to retaliate by whipping him with a towel or something, when the water spread out five inches in front of my face, like it had just hit the cleanest window on the planet, and dribbled to the floor. Not a drop touched me. I started laughing.

"See," he said, "you already forgot about The Shield."

I looked down at the water on the floor.

"Let me try something," I said.

I took the glass from Dad and filled it up again. This time, I held it above my head, and slowly poured it out. I gasped as the cold water splashed down and soaked my hair.

"I guess The Shield assumes that if you want to pour water on your head, then so be it." Dad laughed, and walked out of the bathroom.

As I dried myself off, once again I realized what a strange world mine had become.

✧⟩✧⟩✧

We're not rich by any means, so we all shared the same hotel room. Dad had taken the cash that he had given me for my trip to Utah, which by all miracles I had not lost along the way, and had used the credit card for the rest of the funds he needed to buy us plane tickets and to get the hotel room. The four of us were closer than ever after what we had been through, so it was kind of fun to be in the same room, watching the strangest TV programs I'd ever seen.

It had grown very dark outside and we were all gathered around the television, sitting on the many soft cushions provided by the hotel. The nice Japanese lady had just walked in and given us some snacks and drinks, and we were having a hoot watching some crazed game show where Japanese teenagers were doing all kinds of weird stuff for money. Not knowing their language didn't make any difference.

"This is the silliest bit of nonsense I've ever seen," Mom said. "Surely we can find something more interesting than this to watch."

Rusty spoke up. "Oh, c'mon, Mom. Let's be glad they don't have that horrendous show you watch with all of those fat women talking about nothing."

"Oh, yeah, it's not nearly as intelligent and sophisticated as this garbage," Mom replied. "And don't call people fat. It's not nice."

"Mom, if you were fat, I wouldn't say it. So by saying it, I must mean that you're not fat, which means you're skinny and beautiful, so take it as a compliment."

"That's enough, Rusty," Dad said. "We all know that I am fat, which means that one day you'll be fat, so zip it."

"Dad, you're not fat," I said. "You've just got some cushioning to rest your drink on when you're watching football."

Rusty laughed, and Dad grabbed a pillow and lunged at me. I backed up, laughing, but he was too fast, which was unfortunate for him, because when he jumped on me, The Shield threw him backwards about five feet, and he landed on Mom.

"Alright, that's enough," Mom said, always the calm one. "I'm turning this junk off and we're all going to bed. Tomorrow morning, your dad's going to lay out the plan for getting that dumb old book."

Dad gave Mom his you-always-ruin-the-fun smile. "Okay, okay. C'mon guys, let's get into our futons and get some shut-eye." I always thought it sounded so geeky when Dad referred to sleep as "shut-eye."

"Hey, Jimmy," Rusty said, "Could you maybe sleep with your backside the other direction tonight? My nose needs a break from your reeking stench."

"News flash," I replied, "the smeller's the feller."

"Enough, guys. Go to sleep," Dad said, trying to keep from snickering. Mom surprised all of us when she did break out laughing, and that set the whole room off.

We finally did calm down, although a giggle popped out every now and then, restarting the whole process. After a few more light-hearted insults, we all settled in, and Dad turned off the lights. After such a tiring day, once the laughter died out, sleep was soon to follow.

By then we'd had seven consecutive days of peace and fun, with long nights of plentiful rest.

Well, seven is better than none, I guess.

✧ ☽ ✧ ☽ ✧

I'll never know which was louder or which sound actually woke us all up—the roar coming through the windows of our hotel room, the breaking of the glass, or the piercing scream that came from my mother's throat. None of them were very pleasant.

As we drifted off to sleep that night, you could almost feel the mist in the silent, eerie darkness of the Japanese night. I could only have said this after the fact, but it sure seemed like something was different about that night when we went to bed. We had all been asleep for a few hours when the terrible noises ripped through the air.

I jerked up from my sleep, and a slew of strange sights and sounds greeted me.

The three windows were shattered, and shafts of bright light shone this way and that through the windows, making sinister shadows grow and shrink all around the room. Mom was kneeling on the floor, staring out the window nearest to her, her body a silhouette against the bright lights coming from outside. She screamed only once, but it was enough to rattle an ear for a while.

I saw Dad run to her and grab her, anxiously looking out the windows toward the lights.

There was a constant, terrible scream of noise coming from outside. Engines. It sounded like the roar of engines. Frightened nearly to death, I ran over to my parents, and Rusty soon joined us. Having already developed an instinct from our experiences in the Blackness, we all knew that The Shield would protect us as a group as long as we stuck together. Hugging, we stared out into the night, and right outside our windows we saw the last thing we would have expected to see in this quaint little Japanese town.

Motorcycles.

A *lot* of motorcycles.

✦⟩✦⟩✦

They were everywhere, revving their engines, spinning out, popping wheelies, tearing up grass. They were bullet bikes, the kind that are usually bright colors, sleek, and made to go from zero to sixty in about two seconds. It was hard to get a good look at the riders, but they appeared to be dressed in black, with bandannas flying from all kinds of body parts. It looked like chaos as they rode all over the place, back and forth, narrowly missing each other. And the noise. Never in my life had I heard such loud engines. The sounds pierced the air with violence, making it almost impossible to keep yourself from covering your ears.

But we knew we had to hang on to each other. We knew that these people were not our friends, and it was frighteningly obvious that their attention was focused on our hotel room. They still held rocks like the ones they'd used to break out the windows.

One of the motorcycles pulled up to our middle window, and put down the kickstand. The rider sat there for a minute, staring at us through the dark visor of his shiny black helmet. He finally swung his leg over the seat, stood tall, and walked up to the window. I'm sure Dad was cursing the fact that we were on the bottom floor.

After standing there for a few seconds, the rider calmly pulled off the black helmet. His face was even with the middle of the window, and he stood very close to it, so we got a pretty good look at him, in spite of the fact that the only source of light was coming from behind him, from the bullet bike headlights.

The man was Japanese, with black hair hanging down to his shoulders. He had a bandanna tied around his neck, and one on each arm around his biceps. The bandannas were red, but everything else he wore was black. He had a narrow face, and when he suddenly smiled, we saw that he had white, but very crooked, teeth. I had not seen such a nasty-looking man since I last laid eyes on Raspy.

But nothing was as bad as this new man's eyes. They were as black as the rips I had seen in the Black Curtain. And I don't just mean in the normal sense. There were no whites of his eyes. From end to end, top to bottom, the man's eyes were pitch black. And as he stared at us with those hideous, dark orbs, fear rippled up and down my body.

And then, he spoke.

"My name is Kenji."

His voice was gurgled, like he had something in his throat that he either needed to spit or swallow. He had a heavy Japanese accent. He glanced backwards, arm raised to indicate his fellow bikers, and then he turned back to face us again.

"We are the Bosu Zoku, here to end your hopeless quest against the Stompers. It's over, Jimmy Fincher."

I remembered what it had been like stuck in that tree back in Georgia, that day when all of my adventures first started. I suddenly wished I were back in that tree, looking down on old Mayor Duck. Compared to this new Kenji guy, Duck didn't seem so bad after all.

✧CHAPTER 2✧

A Stick

Dad was the first to speak up after those downright impolite words from this Kenji character.

"If you know who we are, then we know who you are. We thought that all of you pathetic Shadow Ka wannabes were gone, but we were wrong, I guess. But look here, Mister Kenji, you can do what you want, but you must be awfully misinformed. There's nothing you can do to hurt any of us. My boy here is the most powerful person in the world!"

It had just started to sound good until Dad threw in that last part. Not only was it corny, but pretty hard to swallow, especially for me.

Kenji continued his crooked smile and swiveled around to look at his bikers. When he turned back to us, his smile had faded completely.

"Oh, my. Oh, my. I'm so very frightened. Please, have mercy on all of us."

Mr. Kenji was a genuine smart aleck.

He turned around and strode back to his bike. From somewhere on the machine he pulled out a big, black stick before heading back to our window. The four of us remained huddled together, waiting and wondering.

Kenji used the stick to break out all of the remaining glass attached to the sides of the window. Then he put his hands along the bottom ledge, one still holding onto the stick, heaved himself up and swung his legs over. The next thing we knew, we had a strange Japanese man standing in the room with us.

"Let me guess," he said with his gurgly voice, "you have received the First Gift. This is no surprise to any of us. So, what is it?"

For some reason, his question really shocked me. I couldn't decide where he was coming from. If he really didn't know, why would he expose himself by asking us, admitting his lack of knowledge? And would he really expect us to tell him the truth? If he did know, what purpose would it serve to lie about it? It just seemed like a weird question.

Dad decided to ignore him.

"Okay, kids, stand up here, and let's all hold hands. Helen, you take Jimmy's left hand. Rusty, take his right hand. I'll keep a hand on your shoulders, Jimmy. Let's just ignore this freak and walk out of here and go to a police station."

We did as Dad said. Walking to the hotel door, we surely looked as ridiculous as we felt.

Kenji's next words halted us, ending our lame effort to ignore him.

"Don't you want to know what my little black stick is?"

We couldn't help but stop and look back at him. Strange how curiosity works. We all wanted to know what that black stick was.

Kenji stepped in front of us, and then threw the stick onto the center of the floor. It didn't bounce, or roll, or fall over. It was like the stick had been a knife, and he had thrown the sharp edge into the straw floor. But it didn't have a sharp edge. It just landed on end, upright, with the other end sticking straight up towards the ceiling. And it didn't even shake or anything. It just landed, and stood there, perfectly still.

Our curiosity roused, we got a better look at it. It appeared to be polished, black glass, about two inches in diameter and two feet long. And we had no idea as to what its purpose could be.

"Now," Kenji said, "I know all about your silly Shield."

He took out a coin from his pocket and heaved it at my head. I didn't even flinch. It bounced off of thin air a few inches in front of me, and flew off into a corner.

Kenji smiled.

"However, your understanding of it is so primitive. You simply have no idea, little boy, but the Givers are not as perfect as you think. They forgot one little thing about The Shield. Granted, it's subtle, but it makes no difference. The results of their slight will be disastrous for all of you.

"This black stick is called the Sounding Rod, and I promise you, you will not like it. Only you, Jimmy, can set it off—we'll grant you that—but there is no doubt whatsoever that you will. I know you'll try not to, but you will nonetheless—because you don't know how to do it, and therefore cannot prevent yourself *from* doing it. Ironic, eh? Now, take care, and oh, Jimmy?"

I said nothing.

"Whatever you do, don't look at the sun." He laughed. "We'll be there when you set off the Sounding Rod. We will be following you."

Kenji turned around, climbed out of the window, and rejoined his merry group of men he liked to call the Bosu Zoku. With a roar of engines and bright swords of criss-crossing light from the head beams, they all drove off into the dark.

The black stick, unfortunately, stayed with us, not moving from the middle of the floor.

Too bad not a one of us had the slightest clue what this Sounding Rod was.

Actually, we would soon wish we had never found out.

✧ ☽ ✧ ☽ ✧

With Kenji and his bikers gone, we didn't know what to do. Nothing about the strange black cylinder made any sense. In the complete silence left in the wake of the Bosu Zoku, the Sounding Rod just stood there on the floor, sticking straight up, looking like nothing but a very tall and skinny drinking glass.

Rusty spoke in a tremulous voice. "Dad, what's going on? I thought the Giver girl said that we would be safe for a while, that the Black Curtain was blocked."

Rusty was on the verge of crying, which was so rare that it just about made me want to cry too. This made me think. It'd been a long time since I had last cried. I was getting used to always being on the edge of danger and being scared out of my wits.

"It's alright, son," Dad assured him. "Those guys are nothing worth worrying about. Let's not all forget that Jimmy here has a little thing called The Shield, and there ain't nothing in the world that can get to us."

Mom chimed in, "But he said that the Givers forgot something, something that would make The Shield falter."

"Yeah, but he was just trying to scare us, I'm sure." Dad sounded about as confident as if he had just said the moon would start wearing undies tomorrow.

"Actually," he amended, "I should've seen this coming."

"What do ya mean?" asked Rusty.

"I think those people may have a Shadow Ka as their leader. I've tried to ignore it, but now I'm pretty sure I've seen that same black stuff in the sky recently."

"What black substance?" This time it was Mom who asked.

"When I rescued Jimmy in Utah, I was able to find him because I've learned to sense this black haze-like substance that lingers in the air around and above the Shadow Ka and their followers when they're in our world. I have no idea what it is—I think it doesn't really have anything to do with the Blackness or the Black Curtain. That's what I used to think.

"The point is, I've noticed it in the air above Kushiro recently, and I guess I passed it off as the misty weather here, thinking it was just part of the clouds. But now I'm pretty certain that it was the stigma of the Shadow Ka. I think Kenji may be one. Or worse, all of them."

We were all quiet for a minute or two, slowly letting it sink in that things weren't as rosy as they had seemed when we'd gone to bed earlier. I finally broke the silence.

"Well, whatever," I said. "Question is, what in the world are we gonna do now?"

"I don't know," Dad said. "Get some sleep?"

"Are you crazy?" Rusty asked. "How on earth could we sleep after all this?"

"Well, I don't know. Would you rather go to another hotel or what? We have to do something, and we can't survive if we don't sleep, now can we?"

"I vote for another hotel," I said, not wanting to be in that room for another second.

Rusty and Mom both agreed.

"Fine, fine. Get your things together."

No one hesitated for a second. We were in a place of nightmares come true now, and we all wanted to be gone from it, even if it only meant some more peace of mind.

Ten minutes later, we were packed and ready to go. My new Braves hat was firmly in place on my head.

Dad opened the door, and Mom went through first. Rusty went next, and I followed him into the hallway. Dad closed the door as he brought up the rear. After the door closed, we all suddenly remembered the Sounding Rod.

"Well," Mom said, "I guess we can quit worrying about that ghastly thing."

"Yeah, let's go." Dad mumbled.

We started off down the hall. I glanced back at the door, and stopped dead in my tracks.

Everyone sensed my sudden fear, and looked back with me. As possible as the impossible had become in our lives, we all stared in shock.

Along the crack on the hinged side of the door, a glossy black liquid was seeping out of the room and into the hallway, floating in the air, accumulating into a pool of goop right there in the hallway. It looked just like those videos you see of the astronauts on the space shuttle when they're playing around with their drinks, and letting little blobs of liquid float around as they try to catch it in their mouths.

It kept seeping through the crack, until it had all finally come out, and there was a big glob of floating black liquid, shimmering in the air. Then it started to stretch out, and as it did, it seemed to solidify, until before long, we were all staring at the same black glass stick we had seen in our hotel room, defying gravity, hovering without making a peep. What had been a wobbly, floating liquid had now turned back into the Sounding Rod.

Dad had had enough.

He lunged for the Rod, and grabbed at it with his hands. It let him get his hands around it, but then it squirted out in a burst of black liquid, and reformed a few feet down the hall from him. Then Dad swung a suitcase at it, splattering it like a water balloon all over the hallway wall. It slammed against the wall like a glassful of ink, making a huge mess of black goo all over the wallpaper. That sudden sheet of blackness sent chills up and down our spines, because it looked way too familiar.

But after just a couple of seconds, it pooled back together, stretched out, and once again formed the long cylinder of the Sounding Rod, floating in the air, all calm and nice-like.

Its intent was obvious. That menacing little bugger was going to follow us through thick and thin.

Literally.

✧CHAPTER 3✧
Dad's Weird Dream

We made our way down to the hotel lobby, and sure enough, the Sounding Rod followed us the entire way. I began to wonder what other people were going to think when they saw this strange object flying behind us like some kind of UFO. It was late, and there were only a couple of people down in the lobby, but they didn't seem to notice the Rod at all. We were certain they looked in its direction, but they didn't even bat an eye. It seemed crazy, but the only explanation was that they couldn't see it. And then came the real shocker.

There was a huge mirror in the lobby, one of those fancy kinds with a golden frame. As we walked in front of it, we all took a look by habit, and there was no black rod to be seen. I glanced over at the Sounding Rod, making sure it was still there. It floated about four feet from my head. I looked back into the mirror. Nothing.

Not that it was anything new in our life, but this Sounding Rod thing was one strange puppy.

✧)✧)✧

Dad checked us out of the hotel, surprised that the ruckus of the Bosu Zoku had not set off a major panic alarm. People either hadn't noticed or were too afraid to get involved when a motorcycle gang was the culprit. We left the hotel hoping to never see it again and caught a taxi to the train station. We were soon on our way to another town.

Dad figured that we might as well start our journey to look for the book and leave the town of Kushiro behind. He told us all to try our best to sleep on the train, because we'd be on it for about three hours. We were heading for a city called Kitami.

As we settled in for the long ride, Dad opened up and told us some things about the past to give us a better understanding of what we were undertaking. We'd bombarded him with questions ever since we'd escaped The Blackness, but Dad had always avoided them or put them off. It reminded me of my great-uncle Grady, who fought in the Pacific during World War Two. Reflecting on the war brought back such horrible memories for him, he didn't like talking about it too much. Dad seemed to be the same way about his past with the Union of Knights and his search for the key in Japan a decade earlier.

The entire time my dad spoke, I felt like I didn't even blink I was so involved with what he told us. Some of it I had heard before, but it was fascinating all the same.

The man I knew as Raspy was actually named Custer Bleak. Years and years ago, he started a group that was known throughout town simply as a gentleman's club, a place to mingle, play pool, and talk about politics. It was called the Union of Knights, and unfortunately, my grandpa was mixed up in it. Until the day I die, I'll be convinced that his intentions were pure, and that he never meant the group to turn into the horrible thing it eventually became.

We would never know when the Union became corrupt, and turned into the manipulated tool of the Shadow Ka. It may have been that way from the very beginning for some of its members. The Shadow Ka were the army of dark creatures that served as the minions of a terrible enemy called the Stompers.

The Ka were supposedly sent for the sole purpose of preparing the way for these Stompers to come and wreak their havoc. None of us yet knew exactly what that meant, or what they were doing for these "preparations." All I knew or cared about was that the Ka were scary, whether in their human form here in our world, or in their true form in the Blackness—black, beastly, massive, winged creatures, with a piercing scream of anger constantly coming from their throats. To the eyes they seemed like a shadow, but with the substance of a living being.

These Shadow Ka had come to this world and taken over most of the members of the Union of Knights. Whenever and however it happened, we now knew that the entire purpose of the Ka-controlled Union was to stop the master plan of another group, a mysterious people that constantly seemed to avoid explaining themselves.

The Givers.

There was still so much to learn about them. The only thing that was certain was that they were trying to help in the battle against the Ka and the Stompers.

I'd met two of them, assuming there were more than two. The old man, the one I called Farmer, and the little girl, the one who'd opened up one last Ripping in the Black Curtain to get us back to Earth after I'd blocked the Curtain with The Shield. I would never forget the violent mayhem of that blocking—we'd barely survived.

The Blackness was the glue that held it all together, a strange portal between worlds, a marble pathway stretching forever through an inky lake, leading to barrels of iron rings that served as gateways to individual worlds. It was these countless worlds that the Stompers had been spending the ages of time destroying. Our good friend, Joseph, had seen what the Stompers left behind, and it chilled me to the bone. I remembered his description of a sea of beds in a world of gray, holding, as if asleep, those left in the wake of whatever it was that the Stompers did in their quest of destruction.

So much still to learn, so much still to fear. But our part in the battle had irrevocably begun, and my family was smack dab in the middle.

Grandpa had left the Union of Knights, refusing to make my dad get involved at Raspy's request. For this, Grandpa lost his life. To save ours, Dad agreed to go to Japan almost ten years ago in order to find a key that would open a special Door that lay in the woods near my home in Georgia. This Door was placed there by the Givers, behind which was the powerful gift that had ended up as mine. According to Farmer, it was all part of a plan to find a person worthy and capable of taking on the weighty responsibility of leading the eventual battle against the Stompers, when they came to inflict their path of annihilation.

I would end up with that Gift, but that story has been told. The story of my dad in Japan has not, and I would hear much of it for the first time as we rode on that swift and sleek train through the mountains and rivers of Japan.

The Union of Knights realized years ago that their victory would be quick and absolute if they put a stop to whatever awaited under the Door, which they had finally found in the woods of Georgia. Therefore, Raspy knew they needed the key to open it, which according to legends and myths put into place by the Givers, was in Japan.

My dad, because of his knowledge of the Japanese language, and because of his many skills and high intellect, was chosen to go. He wanted to refuse, but had no choice. The Union of Knights had become very powerful in our hometown of Duluth, and Raspy threatened our family directly if Dad would not go.

So, Dad went.

He had nothing to go on, no clues where to start. His trip was financed by Raspy and his dirty money, and Dad stayed in Tokyo for several weeks, spending his days searching the many books and maps of the largest library in all of Japan. He looked for anything and everything that would give him the slightest clue.

Legends, myths, tall tales, cults, unsolved mysteries—anything. When he found nothing, he searched other cities, looking at local information. He went from the south all the way to the north, arriving there in the bitter cold of winter. On the island of Hokkaido, the place where we now rode on a speeding train, Dad finally stumbled onto something.

The locals on the east side of the island were very superstitious, and one ancient myth in particular jumped out and almost bit my dad on the nose. It was rumored that a people from another world had placed something most precious deep inside a fiery mountain.

A key.

A key that would open the door to all understanding, and make its owner the traveler of all worlds.

To Dad, he only needed two words to make him realize that he had finally found something worth pursuing.

Key.

Door.

It had to be it.

Suddenly, Dad had help. Strange men would show up out of nowhere, telling him to go here or to go there, or dropping off ancient maps. The men would never tell him who they were, and they would always disappear as quickly as they had come. Following their advice led him to the strangest place he'd ever seen.

A mountain, a lake, an eerie tower of black stone. The details were foggy to him ten years later, and it had taken all his power to just remember where the place had been, finally figuring it out after the last week of intense study.

He remembered an ancient book in a sweltering, lava-strewn place. He remembered opening the book and reading that he must never remove it from its resting place, or that it would burst into flame. He read another passage in the book that he couldn't remember, and the next thing he knew, he was growing extremely tired, like he'd been awake for days and days.

A compelling force of fatigue overcame him, dragging him towards unconsciousness despite his efforts to fight it. Right there, in the middle of a mountain, with lava all around him, Dad went to sleep on the warm, hard stone.

Once asleep, Dad had a dream, as vivid as real life.

It was a flash of images, only some of which he remembered.

A person he didn't know, his hands against the sides of his head, face in agony, like he was trying to prevent his head from exploding. There was something about the shape of the person that didn't seem quite right.

A giant, hairy creature, passing him in a flash, too quickly to make out any details.

A furious storm, rain and wind and lightning, a woman in white clothing untouched by its fury.

Masses of people, surging through the streets of a city, frantically running from something. Yet they all ran in different directions, in complete chaos.

A view of a sunny landscape, quickly devoured by black clouds.

And then, the most shocking and frightening thing of all.

He had seen me, laughing and smiling, and then an image of me asleep on a bed made of stone.

Dad started to get shaken up at this point, the memories hurling through his mind as he did his best to share them with us. He had awakened with a jerk when he saw me in his dream that day, and when he did, there was a key lying on his chest, the key that would go through many hands until it finally met mine, and opened the Door in the woods.

Dad had barely escaped alive from the place of the book, but couldn't tell us anything more of the story right then. He was exhausted from reliving that year, and on the ragged edge of emotion. He said he would tell us more later, and then fell silent and closed his eyes.

I looked over at Rusty, and he looked like he had just seen five sheep doing a jig on their tippytoes while singing the Star-Spangled Banner, his eyes as big as grapefruits. He returned my look, and just slowly shook his head. Mom said something about how this was all more confusing than *Matlock* and *Murder, She Wrote* combined. I just took off my Braves hat, put my head back and looked out the window at the passing landscape, wondering what all those things could mean that my dad had seen in his dream.

✧⟩✧⟩✧

We had just started to recover from Dad's long story and relax a bit, and Rusty and Mom had already fallen asleep, the Sounding Rod keeping us company, hovering in the air above us, when I caught a glimpse of something that just about made me fall out of my seat.

An old man had been leaning against the door that led

to the next train car, reading a newspaper. I had noticed him when we first sat down. Now, I took another glance in his direction.

He was staring straight at me.

My heart quit beating, and I almost choked on my tongue.

The man's eyes widened in fear, and he quickly dropped his paper and ran out the door onto the other train car.

The world seemed to freeze, and my eyes stared in shock. It couldn't be possible, but there was no doubt. That creepy old man's face had never left my memory. Neither had his crazy eyes and his bummy appearance. It had been such an insignificant meeting, he had seemed like such an insignificant person. I can truly say he would've been the very last person I could have ever guessed we'd see again—anywhere, much less in Japan. But it was him. It was definitely him.

Geezer.

Geezer from Oklahoma.

✧CHAPTER 4✧
Geezer's Message

"Dad, Dad, Dad!" I yelled, once I could get some words out.

"What is it, son?" He asked, shaking himself awake, bewildered at why I was suddenly yelling hysterically.

People on the train were giving me all kinds of weird looks.

"It's Geezer, Dad! I just saw Geezer!"

"What're you talking about? Who's Geezer?"

"The man in Oklahoma! The man at the hotel in Oklahoma who told us about Mom and Rusty disappearing! That crazy old man!"

"What—" Dad looked back in that direction, then swung back towards me. "Jimmy, are you sure?"

I didn't wait to explain anything. I just knew that something wacky was going on here, and I had to find out what it was. I put my hat back on and took off after Geezer, through the door and onto the next train car. Dad yelled at me to stop, and followed right on my heels.

Rusty was snoring.

✧☽✧☽✧

I ran through the door to the adjacent train car and caught a glimpse of Geezer, just as he was closing the far door to the next one. My legs burst forth in a glorious display of speed and I was at the door and through in no time. Geezer was only halfway through the car, continuing his attempt to flee. I ran straight for him, and caught up to him just as he reached the end of the aisle. I grabbed his shoulder and twisted him around to look at me. I did all of this despite the fact that Geezer was six times my age and a foot taller.

He spun around and slammed his back against the door. His face was all scrunched up in panic, and his eyes blazed with fear. He smelled like rotten cheese, and was dirty from head to toe. The nasty clothes that he wore couldn't have been washed in days. But there was no doubt that this was the same old man we had met at the hotel in Oklahoma, the one who had told us all about my mom and brother being swallowed up by the Blackness. My thoughts churned, wondering how in the world this same old fool could be here in Japan, on the same train as me. Impossible. It just couldn't be a coinky-dinky, as my nerdy Uncle Steve used to say.

I was panting from running, but I spat out, "Who are you! Why are you here! Talk to me!"

Geezer coughed, then let out a whimpering moan, the frightened sound of a man tormented by ghosts.

By that time, Dad had caught up with me, and pulled me off of Geezer.

"Just hold tight, Jimmy," he said, "What's going on here? What do you think you're—"

Then, Dad recognized him.

"Oh, gravy. You are the old man from Oklahoma. What the—"

"Dad," I yelled, "I tried to tell you! He's the old man that told us about Mom and Rusty being taken into the Blackness at the hotel!"

Geezer just kept moaning, interrupting himself by mumbling something we couldn't quite make out.

Dad and I stared at each other, letting our breathing slow before we turned to Geezer. Dad held him gently by the shoulder.

"Alright, old man," Dad said, "Who are you? Tell us. Now."

Geezer shrieked, and tried to get away. Dad held him tighter. Geezer gave up, and whimpered again.

"Tell us!" Dad yelled, making me jump. Dad almost never yelled.

"Please, please, don't hurt me!" Geezer said, in his gravelly voice. "I didn't do anything, I swear! I'm only here to give a message. Nothing more! Please, don't hurt me!"

"What message?" I asked.

"The Hooded One! The Hooded One! You must follow The Hooded One! Please, leave me be, leave me be. I'm just an old man. Leave me be!" Geezer then broke down and cried. He shrunk to the floor, and my dad slowly let go of him.

"The Hooded One," Geezer sobbed, "The Hooded One. That's all I know. You must find him. You must follow him." His shoulders shook with grief, and I found myself feeling sorry for him.

Dad and I stepped away, and looked at the sorry excuse for a man, sitting there on the ground, crying like a bullied kid. I felt a deep sadness for the poor cuss, and again wondered who on earth he could possibly be, and what he was doing here in Japan.

Dad began asking him something about The Hooded One, but he was cut off by a huge, hacking cough from Geezer. Then the old man slowly stood and opened the door to the next train. I thought Dad would stop him, but instead, he just shook his head and walked back towards Mom and Rusty.

"Whatever," Dad said as he walked away.

Just before Geezer shut the door, he suddenly yelled out, "The Pointing Finger! The Pointing Finger! You will not find it without The Hooded One!"

Then he slammed the door and I could see him run down the aisle of the next train. I didn't go after him, because I figured if my Dad thought he was a waste of time, then he must not be worth bothering about. I didn't have a clue about anything he had just said, and wondered if I ever would.

As I began down the aisle towards my family's car, I looked up and noticed the Sounding Rod, still floating in the air, still following me around. What a strange life I led.

I sneezed at one point walking down the aisle, and some nice old lady said something to me that had to have been the Japanese version of "bless you." It sounded like, "Kaze ohiku." Weird how life goes on, and people can say, "bless you" in another language and it seems totally normal.

As I headed for my seat, my eyes wandered aimlessly over all the Japanese faces as they rode to their ordinary destinations. They all seemed to keep to themselves, and not even wonder about our little escapades. Maybe they were used to crazy old men sounding off in another language and black rods floating in the air. Of course, it seemed as if only we could even see the stupid thing.

I sighed, and decided I was going to throw all this nonsense out of my head and take a nap in my seat. I was about three steps from my seat, just about to say something to Rusty, when the Sounding Rod swooshed down and hovered right in front of my face, like it had invisible eyes that were staring at me. I stopped, shocked, and stared right back.

The end of it started to rotate, and little flaps started to twist off of it like layers of an onion, like a whirlpool, twisting and twisting until it was obvious that it was opening up. The hole got bigger and bigger until the Rod looked like a long stick with an upside-down cone on the end of it, with the inside of the cone so dark that I couldn't make out if anything was inside the cone or inside the Rod itself. Then, at the very center of the cone, a small light appeared.

Without warning, a sound exploded out of the Rod, high-pitched and terrible. My hands clamped onto my ears, and I screamed from the sudden pain of the stabbing thunder of noise. Others on the train may not have been able to see the Sounding Rod, but they all heard its horrific sound, and within seconds the inside of the train exploded in chaos. The deafening sound filled the air, people screamed, holding hands over their ears, rolling on the ground in the aisles and between the seats. People were running. And I suddenly felt different. Something was missing. I felt very odd.

A Japanese man rushed past me, bumping me and throwing me onto the floor of the train. Another man stepped on my leg, causing me to grab it because it hurt like crazy, only to clamp my hands right back on my ears when the sound exploded through my head.

And then, I knew.

The Shield was gone.

The man bumping me, the man stepping on my leg. That was all it took for me to know.

The Shield was gone.

I only had seconds to ponder this chilling thought before the world around us exploded in a swarm of glass and wind.

✧CHAPTER 5✧

Train Hopping

I never knew that the world could be filled with so many horrendous sounds at the same time. The piercing blast of the Sounding Rod, the screams of the passengers, the noise of people falling and shouting—all were overwhelming. Then it was joined by the sudden blast of shattering glass. Every window on the train exploded inward simultaneously, with a great rush of wind that splattered us with little shards of glass. I realized quickly how horrible it was not to have The Shield to protect me. I could feel the glass grazing my skin all over, and the fear more than the pain seemed too much for me to bear. I squeezed my eyes shut, fell on my knees, and wailed, my hands still pressed against my ears.

Only seconds after the windows exploded, a mass of black bodies flew onto the train from above. It was hard to tell where they came from or how they did it. In every window, a man dressed in black flew through, feet first, and landed in the middle aisle, standing up. Every direction, every window, it was the same. A man in black, with a very familiar trademark. Red bandannas.

The Bosu Zoku.

The words of Kenji came back to me. How the Sounding Rod would soon go off, and they would be there, waiting, ready when it happened. They were here.

The panic of the situation, coupled with the fact that I was now a kid without The Shield, burst throughout my body in the form of adrenaline. I jumped up, while instinct figured out what to do. There was no doubt what these freaks were up to. They wanted me, and they now knew I had no protection.

Everything happened so quickly. Out of the corner of my eye, I saw several of the Bosu Zoku grabbing my family, putting handcuffs on their wrists. My dad struggled, punching and kicking and pushing like a madman. But they were too much for him. They had him down on the ground, and they handcuffed his legs as well.

My mom was screaming, my brother crying. They didn't even try to get away. They knew their situation was hopeless, that they were powerless against these crazed bikers. All of this, I saw in seconds. And then, they were on me.

Two guys in black hit me from behind, knocking me onto my stomach. As my hands left my ears, the roar of the Sounding Rod exploded in my head. I had no choice but to endure it now, and my ears seemed to have grown accustomed to it. I rolled over and kicked upwards, not even taking the time to think or aim. My right foot landed in the best place possible, making one of the guys yell out and shrink to the floor. My left foot landed square on the knee of the second guy, and I felt more than heard a sickening crunch. Amazing what a little adrenaline can do to a guy's kicking abilities.

But there were more coming from either direction. I had no hope, no chance. But I couldn't give up.

I jumped onto one of the seats to my right, across the aisle from my family. I made for the window just as three or four Bosu Zoku lunged for me. They were grabbing me all over the place, searching for a good hold. I just kept squirming and kicking, trying to make it to the window. But they had me.

Then the train lurched, like it had just hit the unluckiest cow in all of Japan. Everyone on the train was thrown forward a few feet, and the men in black lost their hold on me. Without hesitating, I jumped back onto a seat, and reached for the plastic loop above the window, the thing people hold onto as they get up from their seats. I grabbed it and jumped off of the seat onto the window sill, balancing my feet on the thin edge that used to hold a nice big window for passengers to gaze out as they watched the beautiful landscape of Japan.

I turned my body around, so that my bottom and back were hanging out of the train. It was then that I realized that this train was moving dang fast, and the fierce wind just about blew me out onto the rushing terrain. I held on with strength that came from sheer desperation. I was terrified. If I jumped, surely I'd smash against some rocks and get killed. If I went back in, the Bosu Zoku had me. I didn't know what to do.

Then a hand grabbed my leg. I kicked it away, and reached outside of the train, above the window, looking for anything to grab. Half a foot above the window on the outside was a metal railing that ran all the way down the train. I gripped it with both hands, and pushed off with my feet, swinging myself a few feet from the window. Just as I did, a Bosu Zoku grabbed for my legs, trying to hug them and pull me back in. I glanced in shock as he tumbled from the train, smacked against the ground and was gone in a flash.

Confirmed. That wasn't the way to escape.

My body swung back down, and I kicked out at anything I could. I caught another guy in the jaw, and heard him say something in Japanese that I'm fairly certain wasn't very nice. I put my feet back on the bottom edge of the window sill, steadied myself, and then pushed off again, jumping up with my legs to try and hook them around the same railing that I was so desperately holding onto. Another guy lunged for me as my legs swung upwards, just barely catching himself before he met the same nasty fate as his buddy.

My legs found the railing, and I hooked them over it and pulled myself up so that I was even with the railing. This made another guy miss me, and he couldn't save himself. This time, I was glad that my back was to the ground so that I couldn't see his tragic end.

The wind was strong, ripping at my hair and clothes and roaring in my ears with a hurricane force that managed to drown out the Sounding Rod. But it was still there.

Holding on with strength I didn't know I had, I reached one arm over the top edge of the train and felt for a handhold. I felt some kind of metal pole, and grabbed it. Grunting with effort, exerting every ounce of strength in my puny body, I pulled myself up onto the top of the train, kicking and squirming with my legs and body to help. Straining until I thought my arms would pop, I finally was on top, and immediately scooted to the middle, holding onto anything I could find to keep myself from being blown off by the wind.

There I crouched, on my knees, staring forward into the rushing wind, my hair and face and clothes being slapped by the torrent of air. Fear for my family overcame me, dust in the wind made me sneeze, and tears of panic moistened my eyes, only to be dried immediately by the windstorm of the century.

Suddenly, there was a strange silence, despite the roar of the wind. I realized that the Sounding Rod had stopped. With wind trying to eat my hair, I looked to my left, and I saw the Rod float up from the train and hover there beside me, actually flying through the air at the same speed as the train. The black cone was gone; the sound had stopped.

I wondered if that meant The Shield was back. The wind was still ripping at me, but I wasn't sure if the wind was considered dangerous enough to hurt me or what. I couldn't know if The Shield would protect me from wind. It sure seemed like it would, but I didn't know for sure.

Then I noticed that all along the train, ropes were tied to the railing along the top, and were hanging down, flapping in the wind. That must be how the Bosu Zoku jumped down into the train, like a bunch of SWAT team wannabes. And maybe the Sounding Rod was what made the glass explode. My thoughts vanished in a jiffy, because before I knew it, there were hands on those ropes, and I soon realized that a lot of men in black were climbing back onto the top of the train.

They were coming for me.

I wanted to run, but they were climbing from both directions, including one right beside me. What to do, what to do? My head pounded with panic, desperate for a clue of how I could get out of this pickle.

A movement caught the corner of my eye, and I jerked my head to look forward. Coming straight for me was a Bosu Zoku, only ten feet away. He jumped at me, reaching forward to grab me and pin me to the ground. I had no time to move, or anything. I was sure it was over.

But then, time slowed. As the lunging man got within inches, he suddenly stopped, and then was swung back violently, tumbling over and over until he knocked over two Bosu Zoku just climbing onto the top of the train. All three of them fell.

A surge of relief ripped through me from my head to my toes.

It was back.

The Shield.

Why wasn't The Shield protecting me from the wind like it had the cold and snow back in that frozen world in the Blackness? There must be some good to it, something in the wind that was to help me. I barely had the thought before I was surrounded.

They couldn't hurt me because of The Shield. The relief of that thought was like being told by your doctor that so sorry, what we thought was a terminal illness turned out to be a simple case of bad gas.

But a big portion of my confidence had been forever altered. I now knew that The Shield was not all-powerful, despite what the Givers had led me to believe. With the Sounding Rod bound to go off at any time, I needed to do something. And the worst of all—I knew my family was in the hands of the Bosu Zoku, and that there was just no way I could risk trying to rescue them right then because I'd be dead in the water if the Rod decided to go off.

I was surrounded but not in danger. I was all-powerful but powerless. Maybe my head snapped from the pressure, maybe some wisdom I didn't know about took over, but I then made a decision, and acted on it.

Turning towards the back of the train, wobbling in the wind, looking like a drunk man, I took off running. A couple of Bosu Zoku tried to stop me, only to be knocked aside by the power of The Shield. From the corner of my eye I noticed one fall off the train, the other barely hanging on to one of the ropes.

I ran and ran, leaping from car to car like some jumping-bean superhero, not caring about the Bosu Zoku pursuing me from behind. I reached the last train car, but didn't slow down. Instead, I picked up speed, running at a full sprint, straight for the very end of the train and whatever lay below.

I could imagine the shocked expressions, universal to all languages, of the men in black and red bandannas as my wiry little body jumped with every ounce of my might from the back of the train and into oblivion.

✧⟩✧⟩✧

Two thoughts popped into my head as I reached lift-off. First, I realized that we were right smack in the middle of a huge bridge, hundreds of feet above a valley of rocks and rushing water. Second, I sure hoped the Sounding Rod stayed quiet for just a wee bit longer.

✧CHAPTER 6✧
Bubbles and Shields

The direction in which I jumped would have made me miss the train track altogether and fall straight down into the valley, but just as my feet left the train, a blast of wind came out of nowhere from below, strong enough to make me land on the tracks. And that landing was the oddest sensation I'd ever felt.

I once saw a movie about a boy who was allergic to everything under the sun, and had to live inside of a big plastic bubble. Now I'm sure it's not too nice to make fun of people who really do have to live in a bubble, but this movie was pretty funny. That kid went everywhere in the world, and nothing could hurt him because the bubble would protect him. If a bus hit him, he'd just shoot into the air and then come down and bounce a few times but be totally okay. I laughed like a deranged hyena when I saw that movie. But no lie, that's exactly what The Shield was like when I fell from that train.

I had to have been going a million miles an hour. As I fell toward the tracks, I could see the bridge rushing up to me. I tried to get my feet under me, but it was useless. I was heading straight down, front-first, ready to do the biggest belly flop in history. Except there wasn't any water, only steel and wooden railway ties. I closed my eyes and waited for the crushing smash of my skin and bones colliding with the bridge.

But The Shield held true, and inches before I was

smashed to bits, it rebounded me backwards, and I shot back into the air about twenty feet, repelled by the power of The Shield.

I felt like Superman.

I was bubble-boy.

I came back down and bounced again, shot up into the air by The Shield. This time I only went about ten feet up. The next time, five. By that time, I was okay, and landed nice and easy on the old feet. Once again, The Shield had saved my hide.

I caught my breath, allowed the adrenaline to calm down, and sat down on the tracks. The reality of everything that had just happened hit me, and it felt like a million tons of granite had just been poured on my head. My family was gone, once again kidnapped by ruthless thugs of the Shadow Ka. Just because Raspy was gone obviously meant nothing. They were everywhere, and my blocking of the Black Curtain had been a useless waste of time.

My family was gone. For all I knew, they might be dead. I was in the middle of a foreign country where I couldn't speak the language. I didn't have any idea where I was. I had no food. I had no money. I had no possible way of knowing where my family would be taken to, if they were even meant to stay alive. And I certainly didn't know where that stupid magic book was located. I had absolutely, positively not one idea of what I should do or where I should go. The situation had turned hopeless.

Not to mention the fact that I was on the middle of a huge bridge, with another train coming down the tracks, straight towards me.

✧ ⟩ ✧ ⟩ ✧

Shaken from my sad stupor, I yelped like a little dog

and shot back to my feet. You'd think in our modern society they'd build train bridges that were nice and safe with a little walkway for nice boys who fall off trains and sit there and mope until another one comes by to run him over. Who knows how long I had been sitting there, but it didn't matter anymore. I was on a bridge that had nothing but tracks, and I was smack dab in the middle. I didn't need to be a genius to calculate that the train would reach me before I reached the end of the bridge.

My grandpa (on my mother's side) used to say something about a frog and boiling water and frying pans and jumping with fire, or something like that, and I never had a clue what he was talking about. But I had the strangest thought as I stared at this speeding bullet of a train that maybe old grandpa was talking about this kind of hairy situation, because it seemed impossible that I had not noticed the thunderous noise of the train sooner.

Now, I knew that The Shield would protect me. That wasn't my concern. The main thing to worry about was how the train would react when it hit The Shield. I didn't want to be responsible for sending a train full of nice Japanese people to a fiery death in the valley below.

I turned and ran, but this was only a temporary thing. I knew I couldn't make it. But what else was I to do? The only other alternative was to jump into the valley, and I was flat-out sick and tired of jumping off things.

The roar of the train was getting closer and closer. The driver must've just noticed a little foreign boy on his tracks because suddenly a loud horn sounded, and the sound of screeching brakes and the smell of burnt metal filled the valley air. I ran and I ran, hoping against hope that maybe the train could stop in time after all.

I had made it about halfway to the end of the bridge, but

there was still a good football field or so to go. I chanced a look behind me, and the train was rushing up fast, bellowing its horn and grinding its brakes. But it wasn't going one bit slower. I pushed, I grunted, I tried to think myself faster.

My foot snagged on a railway tie, and I flew forwards, face first, and landed on my stomach, right in the middle of the tracks. It didn't hurt because of The Shield, but that didn't matter too much at the time, because the train was almost on me.

Suddenly reminded of the first time I saw a Shadow Ka in the Blackness, I did the crabwalk, scooting backwards as fast as I could down the tracks.

The train was forty yards away.

I got back onto my feet and started to run again. I looked back.

Thirty yards.

I stopped running.

Twenty yards, no sound of brakes. The driver had given up. Today a poor foreign boy would be tragically run over by a speeding train.

Fifteen yards.

I just couldn't bring myself to jump.

Ten yards.

From somewhere within, from somewhere deep down inside of me, from a special place I can only thank my parents for, I found a little morsel of courage, and grabbed onto it with every part of my mind and heart.

I jumped from the tracks, feeling the passing wind of the speeding train brush my hair from behind as I descended into the misty depths.

Yeah, I was really, really getting sick of jumping from things.

✧CHAPTER 7✧

The Riverbank

Have you ever fallen from an airplane without a parachute? For that matter, have you ever fallen through the air even with a parachute? Ever decided to jump off of a building just for the heck of it? Okay, probably not, and neither had I. So I wasn't quite prepared for what it felt like to suddenly free fall for hundreds of feet. It was fun, sickening, exciting, terrifying, and downright stupid all wrapped up into one.

The air whipped against my clothes and me as I fell, still making me wonder about how strange it was that The Shield would repel snow and cold but not wind. My heart was in my throat, and my stomach was somewhere in my brain. I couldn't breathe, and the terror of seeing the ground rush towards me at a million miles an hour was just about too much to handle. It didn't help that the ground was full of rushing water and rocks, not nice things to fall onto from the sky.

But, of course, as scary as the whole ordeal was, deep inside of me I knew that The Shield would protect me.

It couldn't have been more than a few seconds, but it sure seemed like a month or two went by as I fell. As fast as the rushing wind and upcoming ground were, it still kind of felt like I was going in slow motion. Weird.

But then, I hit the ground, right in the middle of the rushing, white-water river and the jagged rocks. I actually felt myself get a little wet before The Shield bounced me backwards, back into the air. This time I went way higher than I had when I jumped off of the train. I flew up and forward down the river a ways, and ended up bouncing a few more times before I finally settled down and landed in the middle of the river.

The Shield never ceased to blow my mind away. Normally, in the middle of that huge, fast, gushing river, I probably would have been swept away until I hit a big rock, passed out, and drowned to death. But The Shield protected me.

It immediately formed a protective barrier around me, so that I was getting wet and everything, but as I rushed down the river it would protect me from sharp rocks or logs or dangerous waterfalls or anything that could hurt me. It was like I was in a circular, rubber balloon boat, bouncing around on the river and having just a dandy of a time.

In fact, once I settled in for the ride, it was the most fun I'd had in quite a while. I even let out a few yelps here and there, and kind of let myself forget what a horrible mess of a life I was in. It wasn't long before I felt guilty that I would even think of having fun so soon after my family had been stolen from me.

Anyway, there I was, rushing down this huge river, bouncing around, going a mile a minute, when something caught the edge of my vision that wiped my thoughts clean. I jerked my head around, looking for what I thought I had just seen. It had only been a brief glimpse, but I was sure that my eyes had just seen something very profound. I knew I had to get myself to the side of the river somehow. I had to confirm what my eyes had just told my brain.

Maybe they had been tricked.

I started to roll my body, and push out and push off

with my hands, trying to slowly move out of the current and towards the riverbank. It was hard, and The Shield kept getting in my way because it didn't want me to get hurt. But before long I remembered that my brain was the boss of that Shield, and it finally let me get a little risky with my hands and knees, so that by the time I finally got myself over to the same side of the river where I'd had the sighting, my body was all skinned up from the roughness and rocks of the river bottom. I also felt ready to collapse from the effort it had taken. White water body surfing was tough work.

I dragged myself out of the river, soaked to the bone like a skinny-dipping sea lion, and plopped down on the rocky shore to get a breather. I looked back upriver to see if I could spot anything, but there were too many trees.

After a couple of minutes, I got up and started winding my way through all of the trees and bushes and fallen logs, hiking back up the way I'd just come. I couldn't help but think how odd it was that I was in the middle of Japan, hiking by a river, soaking wet, looking for a . . .

There it was.

I'd been right.

My eyes hadn't fooled me.

A huge, gangly tree that dwarfed all the ones around it, stood right by the river, like it was the grandpa of every tree in the forest. There was one monster branch in particular that hung out towards the river. From that big branch, two chains were hanging, with a wooden board attached to the ends, tipped at an angle and very old, looking like it might fall off at any minute.

On the board, there was some fresh white paint, having obviously been put there very recently. The paint spelled out some words, and it was those words that had given me a start in the river, but seeing it right in front of me, being confirmed as real, was just too much.

On a riverbank in the middle of Who-Knows-Where Japan, I sat and stared at an old wooden sign, wondering how it could be possible and what in the heck it meant.

✧❩✧❩✧

The sign said:

Jimmy Fincher

enter the fire, turn to the cold
express your desire, you must be bold
the fire will kill you, there is no doubt
the Ice will fill you, the other way out
beware the rift, see it and die
steps be swift, do not turn the eye
you have three days

CHAPTER 8

Another Mansion

I stared and I stared. I confirmed to my own brain over and over that my name was indeed Jimmy Fincher, and that it was definitely painted on that sign. There was no way on earth it could be a coincidence. The odds of there even being a Jimmy Fincher in Japan were slim enough, but the chances of a sign addressed to him by a river that I just happened to fall into were completely zero. I continued staring, seeming to think that somehow that would eventually trigger something to explain this unbelievable sign.

After a while, I noticed something odd on the ground.

Below the sign, there was a little pool of white paint, slowly seeping into the dirt and trickling down to the river. From that pool of paint, there were little drops and splotches along the ground, leading down a path that went into the woods. I figured that meant one of two things. Either the painter of the message was very messy, or he or she, or it, wanted me to follow the trail of paint for some reason. Either way, I decided that following the paint was the only way I'd have any questions answered.

A twig snapped to my left.

I quickly looked in that direction, and just barely caught some movement. There, in the darkness behind the trees, was something that seemed to stand out, a massive shape that didn't quite seem like a tree. Keeping my eyes glued to the spot, I stepped a little closer, momentarily forgetting about the unbelievable sign addressed personally to me.

The shape, the shadow, moved back. With a quick intake of breath, I stopped. Whatever stood there was way too big to be human, and suddenly I didn't care too much to know what it was. I stepped back.

The shadow moved again, and this time something was coming out of the dark towards me, very slowly.

It was a hand, a very hairy hand, a very large hand. Definitely not human.

Losing my breath, I stumbled backwards and fell onto the ground. The hand jerked back into the woods, and with a swoosh of air and moving branches, the shadowed owner of the hairy hand vanished into the trees above it. A path of shaking trees was the only sign of the creature's departure into the dark forest.

Going into the woods no longer seemed like such a good idea. Catching my breath, standing up, I tried to figure out what I'd just seen. It had been huge, absolutely huge. The shape of the shadow in the trees had been more than twice as tall as my dad.

After a few minutes of some pretty intense thinking, I decided that the beast would have come to eat me if it really wanted to, and that there was really no other choice but to follow the paint and see where it led.

Everything seemed to be overloading my poor four-teen-year-old brain, and I even wondered if maybe I'd just imagined it all. I walked over to where the beast had been, and sure enough, there were many signs that a big hairy monster had just been sitting there—broken branches, flat-tened leaves on the ground, the smell of Rusty's bedroom.

Shuddering at the memory of the hairy hand, I collected my wits and went back to the sign.

Courage seeped in, knowing that for the moment The Shield was with me.

I headed off in the direction of the paint, which went into some thick trees, along a narrow worn path littered with roots going in every direction. It was really growing dark outside, so I just knew I'd trip and break my neck before too long. I sure wished I had a flashlight or something.

Out of habit, I reached up to turn my Braves hat around backwards, when I realized that once again, I had lost it. I couldn't remember when, or how, but it was gone. It was probably in the mad, rushing wind outside of the train. I knew it was a silly thing now that my life had become so important and serious, but I felt like crying nonetheless. Wearing a Braves hat was like wearing my arms. I couldn't help but think how hard it must be to find one of those in Japan. Then I told myself to quit whining, and moved on.

As I went deeper into the woods, it got even darker, and I could barely see. The trees were thick with age, and massive branches were coming off in every direction, intertwining and crossing over and doubling back so that it looked like above and all around me were walls and ceilings of logs. It was the thickest, eeriest woods I'd ever been in. The trees were covered in all kinds of moss and dust. I'm no forest expert, but it had to be one of the oldest forests in the world. It reminded me of something out of *Lord of the Rings*, and I half expected an orc to jump out and bite me at any second.

I kept going, walking slowly, watching out for the big roots and low hanging branches. Some of the roots were so big, I had to actually climb over them.

As I made my way, I noticed how quiet the forest was. I could hear every little sound I made, echoing off the massive canopy of branches above me. The darkness, the silence, and the gnarled, ancient trees were getting me downright spooked.

After a while of clambering, tripping, walking, and crawling, I began to notice that a good deal of time must have passed. It wasn't just hard to see, it was sliding toward pitch black. The sun must've set, and I was in the middle of the creepiest place I could think of, following a trail of paint I couldn't even see anymore. But there was something ahead of me, barely noticeable, but definite. It was a faint source of light.

I kept going, listening to my own breath, the only sound in the whole forest. The light began to grow, and I got excited and nervous to see what it was. I tripped on a root and fell face first into a patch of dirt, and let out a startled yelp. The little sound I made was a boom in the silence, and the dust that I kicked up made me sneeze, which was even louder.

Then I heard something whistle past in the air above me, close enough that I could've grabbed it. It sounded like someone had shot an arrow, but it just kept going. I caught a glimpse of it before it disappeared behind some trees, and it really did look like an arrow. Could somebody have just shot an arrow at me? I'd seen some weird stuff, but I couldn't imagine that a Robin Hood wannabe was hunting me in this old forest.

Then I remembered the Sounding Rod. It could've been the Rod that made the noise, but it didn't make sense that it suddenly wanted to shoot through the air like that.

Now really starting to get panicky and scared, I quickened my pace down the path and headed towards the light. Somewhere up ahead I heard the sound of shattering glass. I stopped, and listened.

Nothing. A whistling arrow, and now broken glass. Then

silence. The hairs on the back of my neck were starting to do little dances I was so spooked.

After a few seconds the silence was broken. Somewhere in the distance I heard dogs barking. Lots of dogs. I was positive I'd not heard them earlier. Now the sounds of several dogs yapping away were coming from different directions. Not close enough to worry about any of them running after me like a renegade Lassie, but it was still weird that they all started barking at the same time.

I crept forward, towards the light, and soon came to a place where I could see the edge of the woods, and beyond it was an open area, where the light was coming from. I tiptoed toward the edge of the line of trees, wondering over and over about the arrow-thing and the breaking glass. As I approached the clearing, I stooped down and kind of shuffled my way off of the path and behind a big tree. And then, I got a good look at what was in the clearing.

There were wooden posts scattered here and there around a big yard, and they all held burning oil lamps at the top, flickering in a light breeze. In the middle of the yard was a house. A huge house. A mansion. It reminded me of the mansion I was taken to after Mayor Duck found me in the tree so long ago. The house was still, dark, and quiet, with no signs of life.

No. On the upper floor, to the right of me, there was one window with a light on. I stared at it, trying to get a glimpse of what was inside. I gasped and shrank back when a shadow suddenly passed by the window, gone as soon as it had come.

Someone was inside.

I glanced back at the path, and there it was. Puddles of white paint. I crept over to get a better look. The splotches and pools of paint continued along the path, out of the woods, and into the yard. My gaze followed the direction of the white trail, and it led right to the front door. I knew it was deliberate, and that I was supposed to follow it.

I stepped out into the open.

Another movement above me made me jump, and then I noticed it was the Sounding Rod.

The cone was open, pointing at me, the small light in the middle barely visible. But there was no sound. Nothing. I tried to figure out whether or not The Shield was active, but couldn't tell for sure. Something did feel kind of not quite right, so I had to assume that it was not working, and that the Rod had gone off again.

But where was the sound?

Shaking my head, I decided to move on and find the owner of the paint.

My heart racing, I approached the door, wondering to myself what in the heck I was doing and since when did I have these kinds of guts. As I crossed the lawn, I could see that many of the windows of the house were broken.

As I got closer to the house and the front porch, I noticed that there was a huge white X painted on the door, with writing underneath. The flickering lamps made it look scary and foreboding, and not that easy to read. But I could just make it out, and if I had any doubt as to the purpose of the paint trail, it vanished.

It was written in the same eerie handwriting as on the sign by the river.

Jimmy, come inside

I didn't hesitate. I followed the advice of a sign written by Godzilla for all I knew, and walked toward the second mansion I had ever been so close to.

As I did, I wondered how in the world this person could have possibly known that I would've jumped off of a train and a bridge and end up right here, right now.

The distant barking of the dogs continued as I stepped towards the door. The wooden porch creaked loudly, and the eerie lettering painted on the door loomed in front of me, inviting me to enter. So, I did.

I turned the handle, almost expecting it to be locked, but it opened easily, and I pushed the door inward, anxious to see what awaited me inside. But the house was very dark, and I couldn't see anything. The weight and circumstance of everything suddenly filled me—the train, my family, the wooshing sound, the broken glass, the Sounding Rod, the light in the upstairs room, the barking of the dogs, the white paint. My heart tight with caution, I stepped into the darkness.

My eyes quickly adjusted to the faint light coming from the flames out in the yard, and I could barely make out a staircase opposite the door, leading up to the second floor. The room was up there, the room with the light and the moving figure. Someone was waiting for me. And somehow, they not only knew who I was, but knew that I would jump off of a train in the middle of Japan and float down a river and end up at this very spot.

I glanced to my left and right, but it was just too dark. There was a heavy silence in the house, the kind that is so quiet it seems to have its own type of noise, a deafening stillness. In other words, I was getting creeped out.

I started to climb the stairs, wincing at the sudden noise of my shoes on the wood. My footsteps seemed to boom through the house, and the creaking of the stairs only made it worse. Oh well, whoever or whatever was up there was expecting me anyway.

Step by step, I made my way to the top, and then turned towards the right, where I knew the lighted room was located. At the end of the hallway, I spotted the light coming from underneath a closed door. It was bright enough to help me see what was in the hallway, and the creepiness got worse.

All along the walls, hung randomly with no rhyme or reason, were dozens of picture frames, covering almost every inch of the hall. Some were big, some were tiny, and they were very disorganized. At first, the pictures themselves were very hard to make out. I leaned towards one of the bigger ones, and strained my eyes, urging them to work in the faint light. The picture started to take on a form, and I could see shadowy outlines of people, and then the background, which looked like trees and a building.

I reached out and grabbed the edge of the picture, and then tilted it towards the lighted door, hoping to make out more of the details. It worked. I gasped, sucking in air like a commercial vacuum cleaner, and let go of the picture. It slipped from the nail and crashed to the floor, shattering the glass protecting the picture with a sonic boom. I backed away in disbelief, slamming into the opposite wall. A cascading onslaught of picture frames crashed to the ground all around me, glass breaking everywhere, filling the air with terrible noise.

I looked towards the door at the end of the hallway and saw a shadow quickly flitter past the light coming from underneath. Dread suddenly filled me, and I no longer wanted to go anywhere near that room. I turned to run back down the stairs, feet crunching on glass, when I felt more than heard the door whip open behind me, creating a stir in the dead air of the hallway. I couldn't help but stop in my tracks.

There was no other sound, no voice, no movement after the door opened. I turned and looked back. Filling the doorway was the dark shadow of a man.

With the light coming from behind him, I couldn't make out his face. There was something odd about his head.

I took a couple of steps backwards, scared to death by this new appearance. My hand felt along the wall as I crept toward the stairs, knocking down a few more pictures along the way. And then my hand came across a plastic square, with a strange protrusion in the middle. Only in my present state at the time would my mind have interpreted it that way. It was just a stinking light switch.

When it dawned on me what it was, instinct took over.

I flipped the switch.

✦CHAPTER 9✦

The Pale, White Hand

At first the light blinded me, and I convinced myself that my first impression of the figure in the doorway was somehow due to a trick caused by the sudden switch from darkness to light. But my eyes adjusted in a matter of seconds, and there was no trick.

The man, assuming it was a man, did not move at all. He was dressed in some kind of robe, covering him from head to toe. Literally. The robe had a hood, and it was the biggest hood I'd ever seen. Not only did it cover his head, it drooped down in front of his face so much that all you could see was the material of the robe, which was made of a rough, scratchy cloth that was the color of fresh dirt. The robe itself hung all the way to the floor, so that I couldn't make out his feet either. From head to toe, all I could see of this person was an old robe.

Except for one hand.

The robed figure was holding a hula-hoop. Clasped in his thin, pale, white hand, extending from his hand to the floor and then back again, was a perfectly circular ring, made out of a bright red material, about an inch thick, with the hoop itself about three feet in diameter. He leaned on the red ring, as if he needed it for support. It didn't bend from his weight.

I was looking at a faceless man in a robe, gripping a red hula-hoop as though his life depended on it.

Sudden thoughts of Geezer shot through my head, and I gasped out loud for the third time that night, this time with realization.

Standing before me was the one Geezer had ranted about on the train.

The Hooded One.

✦⟩✦⟩✦

Neither of us moved. A glint of light reflected off the broken glass on the ground, catching my eye. I glanced down, and once again spotted the picture that had given me such fits. Now, with the light from the room, it was much more visible. It had not been an illusion. I quickly scanned the rest of the pictures scattered across the floor, then the ones still hanging on the wall. Still not recovered from the shock of what had been in the picture, I now could only gape in even more disbelief.

Every frame, every single one, from large to small, had the exact same picture—a photograph.

I looked over at The Hooded One. He did not move, still leaning on the red ring.

My eyes shifted back to the pictures, and focused on the largest one, lying on the floor.

It was in black and white. It was an aerial view of a dark, gray room with four beds lined up, all in a row, evenly spaced apart from right to left in the picture. On those beds lay four people, one for each bed. The people were asleep.

Or dead.

Mom. Dad. Rusty. Me.

As I stared, the picture suddenly changed, right before my eyes. The beds were still there, but now the bodies were covered with a rough, gray cloth—the familiar lumps of the head and feet the only things identifying the same sizes of the bodies of my family. Then, just seconds later, the picture, all of the pictures, changed again.

They all became the family photo that hung above our fireplace back in Georgia.

I continued to stare, but they did not change again.

Movement made me pull my head up, looking back to the robed person down the hall.

The Hooded One was slowly walking towards me.

As he moved, taking small steps, the floor creaked under his weight. He used the red hula-hoop as a cane, leaning on it and moving it forward with each step. The whole world was quiet, the only sound that of the creaking boards and crunching glass beneath his feet. I couldn't move.

Closer and closer he came. The drooping hood of his robe swayed back and forth with each step, but never revealed the face behind the coarse cloth. He reached several of the pictures that had fallen to the ground, now all showing my family portrait, and paid them no heed. The crunch of the glass as he stepped on them was loud and disturbing.

Still, I could not move. For some reason, I wasn't afraid. All I could think about was Geezer, back on the train. He had to be some kind of messenger. There was just no way I could've bumped into him twice in one month on opposite ends of the world. Both times, he had given me warnings, or told me to take heed. I suddenly felt certain that Geezer was on my side, despite his complete lack of skill in delivering a message.

The Hooded One, moving steadily closer, was a friend. He was on my side. I knew it.

He stopped two feet in front of me. The entire house was now silent except for the soft sigh of the wind coming through the broken windows.

I could hear him breathing, a faint intake of breath that

sounded above the trespassing wind. He was alive, at least, not some robed zombie.

The silence stretched on, neither of us moving, both of us staring—if he actually had eyes to stare with and could see though his robe.

He made the first move. His right arm lifted the red ring from the ground, slowly, like he wanted to make sure I knew he wasn't a threat. He lifted and lifted until the ring rose above his head. He brought his left arm up as well, revealing his left hand for the first time, which was as pale and thin as the right one. He grasped the ring with his left hand, holding the hula-hoop directly over his head with both hands tightly gripping the red tubing.

He stepped closer.

Our bodies were almost touching now, and I still didn't move. My breathing was shallow, my heart racing in anticipation, wondering what he was doing.

He leaned forward. I looked up. He held the ring in such a way that it was now directly above both of us, encasing us in its circumference.

The thought entered my mind that the ring he held in his hands was most certainly not a hula-hoop.

It was then that he let go, and the ring began to fall.

✧CHAPTER 10✧

The Bender Ring

As it fell, with me and The Hooded One in its center, the air around us shimmered, then erupted into a million red lines, shooting and swirling in all directions, enveloping us like a swarm of long, skinny snakes. The hallway around us melded into the red lines, until the lines were all we could see. I began to panic as my senses told me that I was floating, and the lines spun my mind until I was sure I was going to throw up.

The house was gone, the pictures were gone. There was nothing but red and the faint image of The Hooded One. My stomach was in my throat, and I jerked my hands to the sides, trying to make the madly spinning lines stop. Now they were no longer lines. They were red flashes.

I looked down, even though direction had begun to lose its meaning.

At my feet, I saw green. It was grass.

Color began to shoot up my legs, making the redness fade. I looked up. The red swirling was still there. I looked back down. From my feet to my waist, there were no red lines, only the color of my pants, the green grass, and the bottom of the rough robe in front of me. Then I saw the red ring, ascending up towards our heads. As it floated upward, the surroundings changed with its movement. As the ring rose, it was pulling reality with it, the redness disappearing in its path. I saw hands clasped to the ring.

In a sudden rush of movement, the ring cleared our heads, and the last of the redness vanished. I was again standing in front of The Hooded One, with him holding the red ring above us. We were surrounded by silence. He quietly pulled the ring to the side, and lowered it back down to a position in which he could once again lean on it for support.

He staggered a little, as if he had just gone through a tremendous ordeal. He stepped back a few steps, and collapsed to the ground, too exhausted to stand.

I stared at what lay on all sides of me.

I stood in a field of grass, under a newly risen sun. To my left was a towering mountain, sloping quickly to the sky from where we stood, so that it was almost impossible to see its top. It was a green mountain, heavily wooded with occasional peaks jutting through the trees here and there. Mist hung all about the trees and rocks, enveloping the mountain in a quiet stillness. I thought it was one of the most beautiful things I'd ever seen.

To my right was an old wooden shack, with a rickety front porch, no glass in the windows, and all kinds of plant growth invading the place. It had to be abandoned. Beyond the shack, I could see a descent into a valley, and realized that we were actually already fairly high up on this mountain.

I looked back at my robed friend. He was in a sitting position on the ground, looking up at me, or whatever you call it when a guy points his hooded head at you so that it looks like he's looking at you.

For the first time in what seemed ages, I spoke.

"Mr. Hood, do you talk?"

It didn't sound right when it came out, but I needed to say something, and I needed to know if this guy would answer questions.

He shook his hooded head, a definite "no."

I lost all sense of bravery and slumped to the ground, on the verge of tears.

"Then how in the world am I supposed to know what's going on? Am I even in Japan anymore? What was that thing? Is this a place in the Blackness?"

I had a million more questions, but figured it was pretty pointless to keep voicing them to a guy who couldn't talk anyway, even if he did have any answers.

The Hooded One stood and walked over to the shack.

There were some loose boards, and he picked one up. He walked back over to where I was sitting and sat back down on the ground. He placed the board in his lap, "looked" up at me, and then pointed at the board.

I nodded, even though I didn't know what he was doing.

Then Mr. Hood started writing on the board with his finger.

✧ ☽ ✧ ☽ ✧

I never thought that in all my life I would meet a man who dressed in an old robe, didn't let people see his face, carried a magical red hula-hoop with him, couldn't talk, and could use his pinky finger as a paintbrush. But I just had.

I don't know where the paint came from, it just appeared under his finger as he brushed it along the wood. The paint was white and bled a little, and I now knew for sure who had made the signs guiding me to the house by the river, and how it had been done.

As the words appeared on the board in front of me, I soon forgot that he was using his finger as a paintbrush. I was learning to adapt quickly to things that were weird.

"YOU ARE IN JAPAN. WE USED THE BENDER RING."

"The Bender Ring?" I asked him.

He continued painting with his finger, this time on the other side of the board.

"IT IS MY GIFT. I USE IT TO COMPETE WITH THE SHADOW KA."

The sight of those last two words sent a chill down my spine, and formed a lump in my throat. The Shadow Ka were scary things no matter which form they took—as the winged beasts in the Blackness, with their screeching cry and demented viciousness, or as controlled humans in this world, like Raspy. Either way, I was glad to hear Hood talk about competing with them. That confirmed to me that we were on the same side. Another question popped in my head.

"Are you one of the Givers?"

Hood was running out of room, but he had enough to write the word, "NO."

"Then who are you? How do you know about the Shadow Ka, and how do you have magical powers like that ring thing?"

Hood stood up slowly and walked towards the shack. He looked back and gestured that I should follow. We walked over to a blank wall on the side of the shack and continued our strange conversation.

"I AM A MEMBER OF AN ALLIANCE, FORMED YEARS AGO. WE HAD LEARNED OF THE STOMPERS THROUGH OTHER MEANS, BUT CANNOT DO MUCH. THE GIVERS DID NOT KNOW ABOUT US FOR A LONG TIME. BUT WE FIGHT FOR THE SAME CAUSE. WE ARE HERE TO HELP YOU, JIMMY. EVERY RESOURCE WE HAVE IS YOURS."

He pointed a finger at me, and then resumed writing.

"IT IS NOT MUCH."

"The old man on the train," I said. "Is he one of your group?"

"YES."

"Why are you guys so . . . different?"

As soon as I said it, I realized that I had just said something very rude. I wanted to take it back, but I also really wanted to know.

Hood paused, as if he were thinking very deeply. I worried that I had hurt his feelings, and was about to apologize when he started writing again.

"AS I SAID, WE ARE NOT MUCH. WE ARE THE MEEK AND THE HUMBLE."

He paused again, his head hung low.

"WE ARE THE ONLY ONES WHO WOULD BELIEVE."

I reached out to touch his shoulder, unexpectedly moved by his words. He flinched and pulled back, shaking his hood left and right.

"Sorry," I said, suddenly feeling very awkward.

Hood reached out to the wall and began to write again.

"TIME IS SHORT. WE MUST FIND TANAKA AND MIYOKO. THEY KNOW WHERE TO FIND THE BOOK. THAT IS THE BEST THING WE CAN DO FOR YOU NOW."

At the mention of a book, my heart skipped a beat. I had completely forgotten about it in the madness of the last day or so. With Dad kidnapped by Kenji and the men he called the Bosu Zoku, I had given up on the book. Dad was the only one who would know how and where to find it.

"The book? You mean *the* book? The book from the Givers?"

"YES."

With that, he turned and walked to the back of the shack, leaning on the Bender Ring the entire time.

My thoughts were going a mile a minute. Slight hope flickered in my heart. If I really could be guided to the book, and get the other Gifts, maybe we had a chance. Maybe it would help rescue my family. Maybe I really was meant to be the one to stop the Stompers. I grew more excited with each thought as I followed Hood around the corner of the shack, into the wooded area behind. I stumbled when I saw the man sitting on the recliner.

In the middle of a clearing, with plants and trees all around, with weeds actually growing up the side of it, sat a blue, cushioned recliner, the kind that is perfect for watching football with a root beer and a bag of chips. Except this chair was filthy, full of holes and covered with dirt. At the moment, it was fully reclined, with vines and ivy hanging off the footrest.

The man sitting on the chair, lounging back like he didn't have a care in the world, had to be one of the strangest people I'd ever laid eyes on.

He was Japanese, with long greasy black hair cascading down around his shoulders, like frayed thread. His skin was very dark, as if he'd been tanning for hours a day his whole life. He had eyebrows that just didn't seem natural. They were long and bushy, like mustaches, hanging down the sides of his eyes all the way to his cheeks. His face was also hairy, but there was no organization to his beard. It was bushy in some places, thin in others.

Then I noticed the dress.

At least, at first glance it sure seemed like a dress. But then I realized it was just some sort of old robe, one of the kimonos that I had seen both women and men wearing.

Surprisingly, it was fairly clean.

His feet were bare, and they had to be the dirtiest, nastiest feet on the planet. This man must not have showered in ages.

As I stared at this strange person sitting on a chair in the middle of the woods behind an old shack, a movement by Hood caught my attention, and I was finally able to quit staring. I looked over at Hood, who was painting a new message on a tree.

"THIS IS TANAKA. HE WILL LEAD US TO THE BOOK."

Then the man in the chair spoke. His voice was high-pitched and spooky.

"That's me, Jimmy-san," he said with a heavy accent. "Glad to meet you, my good friend. It shall be a pleasure helping you save the world. GANBARRRROOOOOO!"

With the last word screaming from his lips, he sprang up from his chair and ran into the house that I had thought was abandoned.

The hope that had just swelled in my heart sank back down to my knees.

✧CHAPTER 11✧

Miyoko

I looked over at Hood. He bobbed his head up and down a couple of times, and went to sit on some steps that led up to the back door of the house. Something about his head bobbing. It seemed that Hood had a sense of humor.

I went over and sat by him, wondering what Tanaka was doing in the house, and what was in store for us as he guided us to wherever we were going.

"Mr. Hood, do you have a name?" I asked.

He spread his feet and reached down to draw on the wooden step.

"NOT ANYMORE. I LEFT MY NAME BEHIND WHEN I WAS LEFT . . ."

He suddenly stood up and walked away, his stooped walk revealing that something was tearing him up inside. I decided I better not go that direction again.

"What about the Bender Ring?" I yelled at him, hoping to erase the soreness I had just brought up.

He stopped and looked back in my direction. He walked back and sat down.

He had to use the next step down for his next message.

"I DISCOVERED THE RING'S USES, BASED ON THINGS I HAVE LEARNED IN MY . . . JOURNEYS."

He looked over at me. It was weird how I could not see a face on this guy but the hood had *become* his face. I almost imagined eyes on it somewhere.

He resumed writing, going to the last wooden step.

"I COULD NEVER EXPLAIN IT WELL ENOUGH. IT BENDS THE WORLD. I CAN TRAVEL ANYWHERE WITH IT, IN AN INSTANT. IT IS UNBELIEVABLY POWERFUL, WHICH IS WHY I CAN NEVER TELL ANYONE ELSE ABOUT IT.

"EXCEPT YOU, OF COURSE."

"Well," I replied, "How did you invent such a thing? I mean, if you were to reveal this to the world, you would be a trillionaire. Not to mention the little trick with the finger paintbrush."

"I HAVE MANY GIFTS, SOME OF WHICH YOU HAVE WITNESSED. MANY OF THE ALLIANCE HAVE SPECIAL GIFTS. THEY ARE WHAT SET US APART, WHAT MADE US, WHAT PREPARED US TO BELIEVE."

He was cut off by the sound of footsteps coming from the house.

"Jimmy-san," Tanaka said as he stepped out onto the back landing. Hood and I both stood up to let him come down the stairs.

I was surprised to see that someone else was with him. A girl.

She was as different from Tanaka as I was from Hood.

She looked to be about my age, with the dark hair and dark eyes of the Japanese people. She was shorter than me, but had an air about her that made her seem taller. She looked very mature, and very smart. And very serious. For every blemish that dotted Tanaka, and there were many, there were ten things about this girl that made her beautiful. But she didn't smile, and didn't seem the type to joke with. Her first words proved it.

"*This* is Jimmy Fincher?" She asked, with almost no accent, and with more than a hint of disgust.

"Yes, this is Jimmy-san, the child of the Four Gifts," Tanaka answered.

She stuck out her hand, with a look on her face like she couldn't believe she had to waste her time to introduce herself. I reluctantly shook her hand.

"Nice to meet—"

She cut me off.

"My name is Miyoko. This is my father. How in the world you solved the riddle of the Givers is beyond me, but I guess you'll have to do. I don't want any of your childish questions or complaints as we do this, okay? My father has made great sacrifices to figure this all out, and you must do exactly as we tell you. Our hooded friend here has done his part, leading you to us. Now we are in charge."

She walked away from me, into the woods behind her house.

I heard her voice from the trees.

"Mr. Fincher, do not let my beauty root your feet to the ground. We have to go. Follow me."

I looked over at Tanaka, and then at Hood.

"Is she a real person?" I asked.

Tanaka laughed. Hood bobbed his again. We all followed her into the woods.

✧⟩✧⟩✧

The trees grew closer together as we walked down the path, with branches thick enough to brush us as we walked. Eventually, the trail led to another rickety building, and I could soon see that it was a stable, complete with horses. As we approached the stable, Miyoko began speaking again. Her voice made me long for those few moments of sweet silence we had just been blessed with on our walk through the woods.

JAMES DASHNER ✧ 73

"Jimmy, being from the city, I'm sure you've never even seen a horse before. You'd better learn quick, because I'm not going to be your horse servant for our entire trip up the mountain."

We were taking horses up a mountain?

"Um, maybe you could tell me a little about what we're doing?" I asked.

"We're already running late!" she yelled. "If we're not there in two days, you might as well go back to your old fancy life in America and let the whole world die!"

I couldn't believe she was standing there yelling at me, and it must've really shown.

Miyoko walked up to me, and looked me in the eyes. For the first time, she seemed to adopt a somewhat pleasant expression, and I could sense an apology coming.

"Listen," she said, "I know you already think I'm mean and you've only known me for ten minutes. But you have to understand my life. Ever since I was a little girl I've been raised among people that the world would consider as escapees from a mental institution. How would you like it if your uncle looked like that?"

She pointed over to Hood, and he waved. He actually waved.

"So," she continued, "I'm sorry if I seem short with you. But we've been preparing to help you our whole lives, and now we only have two days to do it. I'm a little stressed."

Then, she hugged me. Now I knew why I had put off the whole girl thing for so long, even though Rusty always told me it was high time I started "liking" them. If they were all like Miyoko, I'd rather wait. Of course, Mom won't let us date until we're forty anyway, so I still had a few years. Under the circumstances, I couldn't understand why I was wasting time thinking about all this.

Miyoko stepped back.

"Are we on amicable terms now?" she asked.

"Uh, yeah." I replied.

"Good. Get on the horse, we've got no time to waste."

With that, she turned and jumped up onto a black horse, with no apparent effort whatsoever. Hood and Tanaka did the same, swinging themselves up onto a pair of brown horses. The one left was also brown. It stood patiently, a saddle on its back.

When I easily pulled myself up onto the horse and grabbed the reins, everyone looked at me in surprise.

"Jimmy-san," Tanaka said with his heavy accent, "You have ridden horse before?"

"Yes. My Aunt Evelyn has horses, and I'm pretty dang good at it. Now which way are we going?"

Tanaka let out his eerie, cackling laugh again, and Hood nodded his big head as if to say, "That's my boy."

Miyoko smiled. "We'll see how tough you are on the narrow path."

With that, Miyoko gave her horse a gentle kick, and headed off down a trail behind the stable. Hood followed, the Bender Ring hanging from his saddle.

"I will bring up the rear." Tanaka said, gesturing for me to go next. "I only ask one favor."

"What's that?" I replied.

"No gaseous explosions, please. I have a sensitive nose."

As he roared his laughter, like a crazed maniac in a carnival, I raised my eyebrows and set off after Miyoko and Hood.

Finally, I was heading for the book.

If I had known what awaited us, I wouldn't have been so eager.

✧CHAPTER 12✧
Baka the Horse

At first, the trail seemed to be leading us deeper and deeper into a dark forest. The trees grew thicker, and as they did, the sunlight struggled to break through the ceiling of leaves, until it all but gave up. The air was filled with noise—bugs, birds, frogs, and other unidentifiable sounds. We could no longer feel the wind since it was broken by the trees all around us. Everywhere I looked, it was green. So many of my present troubles started with a simple trip to a woods just like this one, and it made me feel a little claustrophobic.

Just when I thought we'd have to turn around because there wasn't enough room for the horses to get through, we burst out of the forest into the bright sun. The view ahead of us took my breath away.

We were on a stone landing, with a rocky cliff shooting skyward to our left. To our right, I could see for miles and miles, all the way to the horizon, where the sun was just beginning to head for sunset. It was so amazing, I couldn't believe it was real. It seemed like a vision of paradise. Fields and forests and rivers, in all shades of color for as far as the eye could see. I wanted to sit and stare for the rest of the day.

Miyoko wouldn't have it.

"Jimmy, this is not a vacation. Let's go."

I looked over at her and realized they were all on the

other side of the landing, heading up a narrow, stone path that led off further up the mountainside.

"I'm coming," I said reluctantly. But she was right. This was no time for lollygagging. We had rather important things to take care of.

I clicked my tongue and wiggled the reins, and the white horse trotted over to the pathway. He was hesitant once he got a better look at it, and so was I. But he obeyed me and moved forward. Again, Tanaka took the rear with that clownish smile beaming all the time.

Miyoko wasn't lying when she said it was a narrow path. It skirted the mountainside, gradually ascending up the side of it in what looked like a small part of a gigantic curly-que. The path itself looked to be about six or seven feet wide. To the left of the trail, a towering cliff. To the right, a heart-stopping fall. I was sweating bullets just looking at it. One bad slip and I'd be hang gliding without a hang glider.

Then it came back to me. Quickly, I looked around, and sure enough, just above me, hovering in the air, was the Sounding Rod, following along. I wanted to scream when I saw that ominous cone on the end of it. How in the world did it follow us through our journey with the Bender Ring! I hated that thing, and felt sicker knowing that The Shield was not going to protect me if I fell off the dang mountain.

My poor horse wouldn't fare too well either in such a fall.

After riding for a while on the treacherous trail, I decided to name the horse.

"Hey, Miyoko," I yelled out, "Does this horse have a name yet?"

"Yes. His name is Baka Ga Ue."

For some reason, Tanaka snickered. I looked back at him and he quickly tried to wipe the smile off of his face.

"Hello, Jimmy-san. Nice day, don't you say?" he said mockingly.

"What does Baka . . . whatever-she-said mean?" I asked.

He replied, "It means, 'He who rides my horse, is very smart man.'"

His laughter howled through the air again, and I couldn't help but finally laugh. I hoped he didn't realize I was laughing at him, not with him.

"Well," I finally said, "I don't care what it means, I'm going to use it. Baka it is. Come on Baka, let's go, boy."

That made Tanaka laugh even harder, which I didn't think possible.

He was cut off by the sound of trickling rocks from above.

We all looked up, and noticed small rocks here and there falling from a small crevice in the cliff face. I wondered if it was an animal or something, or maybe just a natural shifting. While looking up, I saw a rather large chunk coming right for my face, and I didn't have time to jerk my head away. In that split instant, I forgot The Shield was gone.

The rock smacked me in the middle of the forehead. Stunned, I lost my grip on the reins. My feet slipped from the stirrups, and I slid out of the saddle, too dazed to grab onto anything. I fell to the ground, towards the edge of the path, towards the edge that began the long descent below.

Right before I hit the ground, one thought flashed through my mind.

Life stinks without The Shield.

✧ ⟩ ✧ ⟩ ✧

I landed on my back, the edge of the path digging into it like a blunt axe. My momentum kept me moving outwards, and my flailing arms did nothing to help. I rolled off the path and slid down the steep mountainside, feet first. A desperate glance told me that the slope soon turned into a sheer drop, with nothing but air beyond. In a panic, realizing that without The Shield I was a dead man, I screamed and tried to grab anything. Rocks and roots and dirt came loose and slid with me as I tried to take hold of them.

My feet went over the edge, and I felt nothing but empty space down there.

My hand caught a sharp rock, and it held. I slammed my other hand onto the same rock, and gripped it with all my strength. It didn't budge, and I stopped sliding. A last assortment of rocks and dirt continued to slide past me, over the edge and into nothingness. I couldn't hear anything landing below me, so it must've been a long way down.

After a few seconds, everything was still again, and the only sound was me, breathing like a sprinter right after a race. My heart wouldn't stop pounding and I couldn't calm down. I was three feet from death, my feet dangling in open air.

I looked up, and I was about ten or fifteen feet from the edge of the path above. Miyoko, Tanaka, and Hood were all staring down at me.

"Are you okay?" Miyoko cried, and I couldn't help but think what a stupid question that was.

"Uh, not really. Do you have a rope or something?" I yelled back, trying not to make my voice too cynical.

"Of course I do, Jimmy. Who would climb a mountain without a rope? Hold on." Her voice made it sound like I had done this on purpose or something. She was gone for a few seconds, and then her face reappeared.

"Here it comes. Don't worry, my father is very strong."

As Tanaka began lowering the thick, white rope, he yelled out to me.

"Ah, Jimmy-san, bad time for playtime, *neh*? You should be more careful!" Then he barked his familiar laugh.

"Yeah, Mr. Tanaka, next time I won't do this on PUR-POSE!"

The rope slid down until it was right next to my hands. I realized that I didn't really want to let go of the rock. I was too scared of slipping.

Holding as firmly as I could onto the rock with my left hand, I let go with my right and grabbed the rope. I twisted it around my hand a couple of times to make sure I had a solid grip, then grabbed it with my left hand as well. As soon as I did this, I slid down another foot or so before the rope jerked to a stop.

"Hey!" I yelled, "What're you guys doing up there?"

"Sorry, Jimmy-san," said Tanaka, "I was just cutting my toenails and I forgot all about you!" Again, the insane laugh.

I made no comment and started climbing. It wasn't much of a slope—it was almost straight up and down—but it was enough to make the climb possible. I lifted my legs until I could put the flats of my feet onto the ground in front of me, and then I used the strength of my legs to help me slowly inch my way upward.

I made it about halfway before the world began to shake.

✧CHAPTER 13✧

The Dancing Mountain

Earthquakes are not fun under any circumstances. Clinging to a rope while hanging off of a massive cliff with a crazy man named Tanaka as your only hope during an earthquake—that is downright terrifying.

I'd experienced tornadoes and hurricanes, but never an earthquake. It was the strangest sensation. Suddenly the mountain seemed to be made of liquid, and waves of power were surging through it in all directions. When those waves crashed into each other, the jolt was thunderous.

Everything around me shook. Rocks and other debris rained down from above. I had to squint to keep dust out of my eyes as I looked up towards my three companions. None of them were looking at me anymore. I could envision them cowering against the cliff face on the other side of the pathway. Thankfully, Tanaka was still holding onto the rope.

Worried that it might be only seconds before he'd let go, I quickened my pace to get back to the path. It was like trying to climb up a ladder on the back of a big van while the driver alternated slamming on the brakes and stomping on the gas. I was sure the whole mountain was going to collapse any minute.

I held the rope with a grip of iron, and kept moving. Rocks were pelting me, raising bruises, and my feet kept slipping as the earthquake jarred the dirt and rock loose all around me. I didn't give up, praying that Tanaka wouldn't either.

I was three feet from the edge.

The rope came loose. I didn't know what happened to Tanaka, but whatever he was doing, he wasn't holding the rope anymore.

Time seemed to freeze, just like it does in the cartoons when the character runs off a cliff and looks down before he finally begins to fall. Since my legs were pushed against the cliff, with me leaning back, holding onto the rope, the momentum of my body made me begin to fall backwards, with no way for me to grab anything on the mountain to stop my fall.

Some sort of strange instinct took over. In an absolute split second, I made the decision to actually kick out with my legs. As I did so, I swung my arms as hard as I could over my head and back towards the ground. The force of my leg-kick combined with the swinging of my arms caused me to do a back flip. My legs swung over my head and back down. My arms and head spun until suddenly I was facing the mountain again.

I only had one chance.

The same rock I had caught before was right in front of my face.

I reached out and grabbed it.

My body slammed against the cliff.

I held on.

Gasping in air, I couldn't believe what I'd just done.

The mountain continued to shake.

Now I felt like I was on the inflatable tube behind the boat at the lake, my dad constantly going over his own wake to try and shake me off. Somehow, someway, I held on to that sweet, blessed rock.

Abruptly, the earthquake stopped. Debris trickled down all around me, slowly dying out. Then all was still.

The silence that followed was deafening.

I looked up.

Tanaka's face appeared. For the first time, his face didn't have a smile on it. He looked like he'd just been through a terrifying earthquake.

"Jimmy-san! Jimmy-san! Thank the Maker you still alive! I'm so sorry, Jimmy-san! I'm so sorry! A rock hit me in the head!" His frantic voice was filled with relief that I wasn't a pile of goo at the bottom of the mountain. Even when terrified, his voice sounded funny.

"It's okay, Mr. Tanaka. It's okay." I was barely able to get the words out, and I didn't even know if he'd heard me.

"I will get my rope!" he yelled before disappearing again.

We went through the same process again. He dropped the rope. I grabbed it, and once more started my ascent. I had almost no strength, but there was no other choice. Somehow I held on, and somehow I climbed.

When I was just a couple of feet from the top, four hands reached down, grabbed my shirt, and hauled me up onto the path.

I landed on my back, panting, and stared up at three faces (well, two faces and a droopy hood).

"Thank you," was all I could get out.

It was then that we heard the thundering sound.

✧CHAPTER 14✧

Galloping

It came from directly above us—a rumbling roar. Everyone forgot about me and looked up toward the noise. We could see a gathering cloud of dust way up in the air, on the mountain, and it seemed to be rushing our way.

The shrill sound of Miyoko's scream suddenly filled the air around us.

"MUDSLIDE!"

The others reacted immediately, and I decided I'd better follow suit.

They ran to their horses, jumping on and kicking them into action. No one worried about the few things they had bothered to unpack. Although exhausted, I ran to my horse and scrambled for the stirrup. The dreadful sound of the mudslide tore through the air, sounding like a massive thunderstorm falling from the sky.

Kicking Baka into action, I looked upwards as my horse began galloping down the path.

An enormous mass of rock and mud were right above us, coming down like a huge arrow, with its point almost on us, its sides gradually declining behind it up the mountain. I looked back ahead of me. To go this fast on such narrow, shaky ground was incredibly dangerous, with death waiting for us just a few feet to the right.

But an even more certain death was coming from above, so we had no choice.

I leaned forward in my saddle, standing on the stirrups, urging Baka to go faster. I was about thirty feet behind Miyoko and the others, all of us pushing our horses to the limit, hoping they didn't stumble on the rocky ground.

The roar of the slide was deafening. It was on us.

Behind me, I heard a loud boom as the front point of the mudslide slammed into and obliterated the path, gaining more ammunition for its deadly descent. I risked a look behind me, scared it would be my last glimpse in life. *Where was my Shield?* I screamed inside my head.

The slide was crashing into the path in a wave, just like a big surfer's wave gradually falls into the ocean in all the movies. After the arrow point crashed into the outcropping path, its trailing sides crashed into it soon after, in an orderly fashion, like a wave extending from the place where the point hit. It was like a giant was walking along the mountain above us, slowly pouring out mud and rock from a huge cup as he walked along. That torrential downpour of destruction was heading for us, coming faster than our horses could gallop. No matter how hard we pushed, it would be on us soon.

I looked forward, trying to make the horse faster by thinking it could go faster.

It didn't work.

My horse was running with all his strength. I could hear his heavy breathing even amidst the thunderous sound of the mudslide. I was thankful my aunt had taught me how to hang onto a horse so well.

I looked back again. The crashing wall of rocky mud was getting closer and closer. I looked down at the ground and I could see that the force of the slide was already starting to spread forward and wreak havoc on the trail under me. It was shaking and cracking, dust and rocks spitting up from the ground.

All I could hear was the roar of the mudslide, the crashing of rock against rock, the pounding of the destructive wave gaining on us. The others were well ahead of me, their horses quicker than mine. I screamed at Baka to run faster, screamed to the others, screamed for no reason other than out of fright.

A big rock whisked past my head, just missing me. Globs of mud and dust pelted me. Another rock flew past, then another. The dust was cutting off the light.

I looked back.

My vision was filled with a wall of earth.

In a last fit of panic, I prepared to die.

And then, something unbelievable happened.

A small, insignificant thing. A thing that happens to all of us from time to time. A thing that almost seemed absurd. A thing that saved my life.

I sneezed.

✧))✧))✧

Suddenly, nothing was hitting me. There was a strange hollowness to the sound of the mudslide. I looked up.

Rock and dirt were falling on top of me, crashing down with enormous force. But just above me, the mudslide was parting and then going around me and the horse, like we were in an invisible bubble.

The Shield was back.

Thank goodness, The Shield was back.

It expanded to protect the horse, just like it had in the past for my family when they were in contact with me. Baka kept moving forward, at a full gallop, The Shield forming a protective bubble around us.

Having lost confidence in The Shield now, I still leaned

forward, scared, knowing if The Shield gave out again I was dead.

The mudslide was still moving forward in its wave, fully on top of us and ready to pass on by. If it got ahead of us, I didn't know what would happen. Would it push dirt out of our way? Would the slide take the path with it, making me go through another long fall, hoping I'd bounce to safety at the bottom?

I would never know.

Just as the falling earth reached the point of Baka's nose, it began to lessen, and before we knew it, it had died out, and it was all over. Bursting completely clear of the debris, we surged ahead, not stopping. I wanted to put as much distance as I possibly could between the landslide and me.

We galloped on for another couple of minutes, rounding a bend in the mountain, until I could see the rest of the group ahead of us, resting on the trail, looking back with anxious worry to see if we were alive. The looks on their faces brightened with relief when we turned the corner that had hidden the last tense moments from their view.

Baka reared to a stop right in front of them, nostrils flaring.

My last ounce of adrenaline spent, I fell from the horse, exhaustion overcoming me.

Tanaka's famous laugh didn't even faze me.

I was asleep before I hit the ground.

✧❩✧❩✧

Later, somewhere in that world between sleep and wakefulness, my thoughts spun. I thought of several things at once.

Kenji told me that the Sounding Rod would only release

its power when I did something to set it off. I assumed, then, that I also had to be the one to make it stop.

I knew it had gone off once, on the train. And then it had stopped sometime when I was on top, escaping. Then, despite the lack of sound, it had obviously gone off again back in the woods by the mansion.

That awful sound—I had not heard it since leaving the train.

The swooshing sound. The breaking glass. The dogs barking. Somehow it was all related.

Finally, the sneeze. It absolutely could not be a coincidence. The Shield had expanded around Baka and me immediately after I sneezed. Immediately.

I tried to think of the train. What happened on the train? Did I sneeze? Did I sneeze while on top of the train? Did I—

Yes. I remembered sneezing when I fell on the path in those woods by the river.

Could it be possible? I knew my life had gotten a bit outrageous, but this was . . .

Sneezing. Kenji's smart aleck comment back at the hotel came to mind, when he said not to look at the sun. Mom had always told me that that when you have a feeling like you need to sneeze, but can't quite get it out, look at the sun, and that will make you sneeze.

It had to be. The thing that set off and stopped the Sounding Rod was me. Every time I sneezed. But what about the terrible, piercing sound . . .

With these thoughts cycling and bouncing around like a pinball in my head, I drifted back into a deep sleep.

✧CHAPTER 15✧

The Weird Barn Dream

I awoke to the sound of hyenas and the smell of feet.

After a few seconds of grogginess, I realized it was just Tanaka.

He was gently nudging me, urging me to wake up. He muttered that we needed to get moving. It turned out that we had all taken a rest for a couple of hours, which was much needed after what we'd just been through. After a short meal, courtesy of Miyoko, we were off again.

The trail that hugged the mountain got steeper and steeper. Eventually, we came to a small clearing, and Miyoko proclaimed that we would have to leave the horses there and hoof it ourselves. I'd grown so attached to Baka, I was saddened by the thought. We cleaned them a bit, left tons of food for them, and said our good-byes, even though horses don't talk.

After another short rest, we started up another trail, this one winding its way straight up the mountain. It was more climbing than hiking. We constantly had to lean forward to grab rocks and plants and pull ourselves up. My arms and legs were burning from the effort, and I frequently looked up, hoping that the awful slope would level off soon. Hood had strapped the Bender Ring to his back with some loose cloth.

After two solid hours of hiking, our trail finally flattened out into an even area of outcropping rock. We all crumpled to the ground and looked off to the horizon. The sun was already so far down that we could only see the remnants of its light. Night was upon us.

Tanaka and Miyoko had brought some blankets, but most of them were left behind in our scramble to escape the mudslide. Miyoko told us that we would be rising way before dawn, because we just didn't have much time. So, we made do, and settled down for a few hours of sleep. In my condition, I don't think blankets or pillows would've made the slightest difference. Once again, I slept.

✧)✧)✧

The day is sunny, and that familiar smell of crops hangs in the air. I love that smell, especially since it means we are at Grandma's house. I am standing behind the farm-house, looking out at the fields, admiring the gentle waves that wash across them as the wind blows. I can't think of one thing in the entire world that is more relaxing. To add to it, the sounds of the birds fill the air as well. I have never felt more content.

Then I hear a sound from the barn out in the fields, a terrible sound.

Before I know it, I am running.

Plants whip my feet as I run, grasshoppers flee my path, jumping and flying in all directions.

I run harder. I have to reach the barn.

Panting, out of breath, I round the corner and am there, the huge front door of the barn standing open. Quickly, I run inside.

Hay, tools, a tractor, all of your typical farm-things are inside. Nothing unusual.

Then, the sound again. A small child.

I look up into the loft, and there he is. A boy, about three years old. How in the world he had gotten there, and how he had managed the rickety old ladder, I'd never know.

He is crying.

Then, the smell of smoke.

I look to my left. The entire barn is on fire. How had I not noticed that?

Impossible.

I climb the stairs, and grab the boy. He is scared silly, whimpering, his face ashen.

I pick him up, and go back to the ladder. I peer over the edge.

Below us, there is no longer a burning barn.

It had all turned into a fiery pool of lava.

I run down the side of the edge of the loft, looking frantically for a way out.

I trip.

Slamming down on the hard wood, which is hot from the sweltering heat coming from below, I drop the boy. I try desperately to grab him, but it is too late. He falls over the side. I lean over, sick with despair, frantically looking down.

As he falls toward the lava below, I do the strangest thing.

I ask him a question.

"What is your name?" I yell to the falling boy.

"Jimmy," is his reply.

I scream.

✧ ☽ ✧ ☽ ✧

I bolted up from sleep, looking around in a panic. I was panting and sweating like an overweight clown in a Fourth-of-July carnival. It was dark, and everyone was still asleep. A dream. Of course, a dream.

I fell onto my back and looked up at the silhouette of the mountain against the stars. What a dream, what a horrible dream. It reminded me of one I'd had way back in Raspy's mansion. That seemed like years ago, now.

I rolled over and tried to forget about it, but the image of it kept coming back again and again. Eventually it faded, but I never fell back asleep.

Later, keeping her word, Miyoko rose to wake us.

It was way before dawn.

✧CHAPTER 16✧

The Missing Robe

The first thing we noticed was that Hood was gone.

In the chilled darkness of the misty night air, we scoured the area, looking everywhere, calling out, seeking any sign of him. There was nothing. A blanket lay where he had slept for the night, with a small pillow the only other sign he had ever been there. Hood didn't have many belongings other than the Bender Ring, which he never let out of his sight. The Ring was gone as well.

Later, as the first trace of dawn began to illuminate the sky above the mountain, we gathered back together, giving up. Miyoko was the first to take charge.

"Well, I can't imagine what he's doing, but we have wasted enough time already. We must move on."

"Wasted?" I asked. "Trying to find our friend is a waste of time to you?"

"Jimmy, spare me the loyalty lesson, okay? What would you suggest we do? We have until tomorrow to find your precious book. Shall we continue looking for The Hooded One even though it is obvious he is gone?"

I just shrugged my shoulders, realizing she was right. Hood could take care of himself with that Bender Ring anyway. He'd probably used it to get away and was nowhere near us.

"So," I said, "how do you know we only have until tomorrow? Are you telling me that if my family had waited another few days to come to Japan it would've all been for naught? The book would've been destroyed?"

"Whoever said the book would be destroyed?" she replied. "All we said is that you have to *enter the fire* by tomorrow, or your chance will be lost." She walked up to me, her face set in stone. "We don't even know what that means."

"What? You're my guide and you don't even know where you're leading me or why?"

"Jimmy, we are an old alliance. My father and The Hooded One and others you don't even know about have spent their entire lives researching and discovering things that would help the Givers and eventually the Giftholder— you. A terrible day approaches, and we are here to fight the evil that comes. You need to trust us.

"We know where the book is. We know you have to go there. We know that you must solve the riddle of ice and fire. We know it must be done by tomorrow. We know that members of the Alliance used their gifts to find you and bring you to us. It has all worked out so far. Now let's go."

"Why does everyone get on my case when I try to understand things?"

"That's the problem," she said. "There is still so much that we all fail to understand. We must work with what we have. That's why we must go, now."

She reached over to me and took my hand, and gave it a squeeze. I froze, feeling my face and ears go red. Then she walked away, intending for us to follow.

Once I caught my breath and willed the goose bumps away, I set off in her direction, having to jog to catch up.

The maniacal laugh of Tanaka filled the air.

✧)✧)✧

We spent the entire day hiking. It seemed impossible that the mountain could just keep going up and up. I kept thinking we would soon turn a bend or go over a big rise in the mountainside and there would be the peak of the mountain, with a sign that said, "Looky there, you made it to the top!"

But no such luck. Every new sight just brought more mountain to climb.

In some places, the going got pretty treacherous. At one point, we crossed a narrow span of rock that stretched across a deep, misty ravine. It seemed an unreal specter of fantasy, this massive dent in the mountain, hidden under the mist, with a natural dam of stone crossing its path. At times the crossing was only three or four feet wide, and I had to concentrate not to look to either side and just put one foot in front of the other. For some reason, heights meant nothing to me when I was climbing a tree, but this was giving me the heebie-jeebies.

It was slow going to ensure no one fell to their death, but we eventually made it across. After a quick lunch, more steep climbs up the mountainside followed, and by the time darkness began to fall, I was ready to collapse and never walk again.

"When will we stop?" I asked Tanaka at one point, like a child from the backseat on a cross-country drive.

"Oh, Jimmy-san, poor little funny man. We almost there. You need it, just ask, and Uncle Tanaka will carry you, *neh*?"

His laugh followed, way out of proportion to the humor level of his joke.

"If we get to the point where you have to carry me," I returned, "we might as well lay down and send a card to the Stompers, inviting them to come and destroy us. I bet you couldn't carry a package of cheese with those puny arms of yours."

"Oh, that so, American tough guy?"

Before I knew it, Tanaka had jumped at me like a lion, whipped me up in his arms, and held me high over his head like a weight lifter. Then, he started to spin in circles, roaring his laughter, while I felt the puke machine rumble in my stomach.

"Okay!" I cried out. "Let me down!"

Tanaka gently set me down, folded his arms, and stared.

The Shield must have known that I needed that.

Despite our circumstances, I couldn't hold back. I started laughing uncontrollably. I hadn't laughed so hard since . . . since before I climbed that tree on that fateful day. I laughed and giggled and snorted until I had to sit down. Of course, anything makes Tanaka laugh, so he joined right in, sitting down right next to me. There the two of us sat, holding our stomachs, laughing like crazed clowns.

Miyoko walked back to us when she noticed we had stopped moving, and stared at our display. And, in one of the biggest surprises of my life—which is obviously saying a lot—she joined right in, her gentle laugh a refreshing contrast to her nutty father's.

It didn't last forever, but while it did, I felt alive again, and it was wonderful.

✧ ☽ ✧ ☽ ✧

When we finally calmed down, Miyoko announced in a composed, no-nonsense voice that we had arrived.

"Arrived?" I asked.

"Arrived. We are at the lake of the Pointing Finger." She pointed ahead, towards a break in the surrounding trees.

Excited, I scrambled to my feet and darted for the opening. As I neared it, I could see that beyond the trees there was nothing but the distant horizon. I slowed, realizing that I was about to run straight off a cliff. Coming to a halt on the lip of the cliff, between two pine trees, I stared below me in wonder.

We were finally on top of the mountain, or at least the uppermost portion of this part of the mountain range. Stretching out below me was a huge crater filling the entire area of the mountain top, surrounded by lush, green plants and trees. Filling the crater was the darkest water I had ever seen, a deep, foreboding lake that showed no sign of life or movement. Covering the lake here and there were wispy areas of mist, slowly migrating towards me. The sun was well on its way to setting now, and the eerie glimmer of the twilight on the water made me want to shrink away and never come back. I was looking down on a lake that had to be haunted.

A large area of mist in the middle of the lake drifted slightly, revealing something I couldn't believe I'd not noticed right away. In the very center of the black lake, jutting toward the sky as if ready to launch for the moon, was a huge pillar of rock, as black as ink. It had a shine to it as well, as if it were some kind of black diamond or crystal. In places, the setting sun cast a red hue to the rock, and it almost looked like blood. It was not a place of cheer.

The rock was massive, but it was hard to tell exactly how big because there was nothing down there to compare it with. I looked down and realized that the cliff was not as steep a descent as I had first thought, and there was a trail heading from near my feet down to the water, maybe fifty feet below.

I shifted my gaze back to the towering, black pillar.

I didn't need to ask.

The Pointing Finger.

Tanaka came up behind me, and put his arm on my shoulder.

"Jimmy-san, quite, ah, magnificent, *neh*?"

I was sure he was going to make a lame joke about The Pointing Finger picking a huge nose or something, but luckily he refrained.

"It's awesome," I said, "but it's a little spooky. With that murky water, and that mist, and that black tower of rock. Kind of gives me the creeps."

"I have been here before, many times," Miyoko said, stepping up to stand beside me, looking out at the lake. "But I have never been to the Pointing Finger. There was never a reason to, before. But my father, Tanaka, he has been in the Finger, has been in the depths of that place."

I glanced at Tanaka, surprised that he actually had been on, or in, that thing.

"I was not alone, *neh*?" he said. "I had good friend along, one who looks just like you, Jimmy-san." He gave me his big smile, exposing his less-than-delightful teeth. He was the first man I'd met that spewed forth bad breath just from smiling.

"You brought my dad here, didn't you?" I asked.

"No!" he said, a little too cheerfully.

He saw my obvious confusion.

"I just followed him, to see where he ended up. I was very sneaky, like a mousetrap!"

Poor Tanaka had a long way to go with English.

"There is a small clearing down this trail, by the lake,"

said Miyoko. "We will sleep there tonight, and tomorrow we will visit the Finger. Come."

She started down the path. Tanaka and I followed.

After eating some of the last remnants of our food and sharing some meaningless small talk, we all settled down to get some sleep. Despite the million things pumping through my head, sleep came easy.

The day that would come with the dawn was one that I would never be able to forget.

✧CHAPTER 17✧

The Low-Budget Raft

I woke up looking at a dark sky, but it was definitely morning. Gray, almost black clouds filled the sky above us, the threat of rain almost certain. By the time we were all up and about, the first drops had begun to fall. The cold air added to the miserable feeling. Wet, cold, hungry, and tired would be the order for the day, it seemed.

Food was running short, but Miyoko figured out some things to eat, and we all groggily munched and built our strength, with a heavy sense of anticipation hanging in the air like wet cotton. I had no clue what lay ahead of us, but I knew it would be a big day, and fear and anxiety made it hard to maintain an appetite. Glancing over at the Pointing Finger, almost invisible in the drifting fog, I wondered what was up there, or in there, or down there. At the moment, it certainly didn't look inviting.

After breakfast, Tanaka showed us where he had hidden a raft under some old branches, in a small bay near the place we had spent the night. Calling it a raft was generous, because it was the shabbiest excuse for a boating vessel I'd ever seen. It consisted of ten to fifteen logs, strapped together with rope. Tanaka pulled out of the bushes a long, wooden stick with a paddle tied to the end of it with the same rope used on the raft.

"Not much budget in your little Alliance, is there?" I asked.

They didn't laugh, so I figured they either didn't get it or thought I was being rude.

"Jimmy-san," Tanaka said, ignoring my comment, "I spent my childhood near many lakes and rivers. I am very skilled, you will see!" He beamed with pride. I wondered what Tanaka would have thought of my adventure on the boat with Hairy, right before I saw it disappear into the Blackness. My thoughts continued churning, wondering what Monster, Mayor Duck, and Hairy were doing in that frozen world they had escaped into when I blocked the Black Curtain. I hoped they were freezing their tails off.

Miyoko snapped me out of my day-dreaming.

"Shall we go? Jimmy, the book awaits you. The riddle of the ice and fire awaits you. The Second Gift awaits you. Shall we?"

"Wait," I said, "What do you mean, the Second Gift? What do you know about it? What about the other Gifts? How much do you guys know—are there things you're not telling me?" I really wanted some answers.

"Jimmy," she replied, "I have told you that I don't know much more than you. The book is in the Pointing Finger. Surely you know that the book is your path to obtaining the Second Gift. As for the other two, I know nothing. Now come on, let's go."

When Miyoko turned to leave, she stiffened, then screamed, the sound of it finally knocking every last bit of sleepiness out of our bones.

Tanaka and I jerked our heads in the direction of her gaze, and saw what had startled her.

It was a man that we all knew could travel with a hula hoop and paint with his finger.

Hood was back.

And he was not in good shape.

✧⟫✧⟫✧

Hood stumbled along the shore of the lake, sometimes falling and picking himself up. His robe was filthier than before, which was saying a lot, and there were signs of a scuffle, with small rips here and there. Not enough to reveal what Hood was like underneath the robe, but it looked as though he'd been attacked. His pale hand still hung from one of the robe's sleeves. But what stood out the most was what was missing. The Bender Ring. He didn't have it.

We all ran to him. Tanaka and I grabbed him by the arms and helped him walk the rest of the way to where the raft rested against the shore. We sat him down on the ground, and the questions started pouring out, all of us anxious to find out what had happened to the poor guy, and where his Ring had gone to.

He wouldn't answer. Hood kept waving his arm in such a way as to tell us that he didn't want to talk, or in his case, write. Miyoko had even brought over a piece of driftwood for him to write on with his magical finger. But he refused.

"What in the world could've happened?" I wondered aloud. Shrugs were all I got back. Hood just sat there, his head drooping even more than usual. His posture spoke of utter exhaustion, ready to collapse and sleep for a week.

We let him rest for a minute, and brought him food, which quickly disappeared under the hood of his robe, his pale hand a flash of white appearing and disappearing. After a few minutes, we tried again to get the story out of him, but he again refused, more forcefully than before. The man must have been through a nightmare.

"Hooded One," Miyoko said, "Our time is short, and we cannot wait here any longer. Are you well enough for the trip to the Pointing Finger? Do you want to join us or stay here and rest?"

Hood quickly put his hand out and started nodding his head as he rose from the ground and pointed at the raft. He wanted to go.

"Okay, then." Miyoko helped him this time, gently guiding him onto the large, flat raft and setting him down. Hood folded up his legs and sat, crossed hands in his lap, staring out ahead toward the Finger. We exchanged glances. Hood was ready to go.

"Ganbarrrrrrro!" Tanaka yelled, and jumped onto the raft, almost causing it to shoot out into the lake.

"What does that mean?" I asked Miyoko, hearing its annoying ring burst again from the old man's mouth.

"It's sort of a rally cry, a call of encouragement. My father rather likes the word."

"I noticed."

As the two of us followed Tanaka onto the raft in a more orderly fashion, my stomach turned inside out. We were actually headed for things that had not really seemed . . . real. I knew we were going for the book and everything, and that it was how I hoped to get the other Gifts, but now that it was upon us, I was sick to my stomach with nervousness. I felt like I was right back to being that boy in the tree, scared senseless, seeing a man attack a woman and then having her disappear right in front of me.

The dread stirring around in my gut made me want to throw up.

I helped Tanaka push us out into the lake, and it was soon obvious that his driving skills would only contribute to my nauseous feeling. We were less than thirty feet from shore when I finally leaned over the edge of the raft and let it out.

There must have been something left in the old chute, because it would not be the last time I spewed that day.

Sitting back when I was finished, ignoring the others' looks, knees to my chest, arms wrapped around my legs, I let out a big sigh, looking out at the Pointing Finger in anticipation.

I felt much better.

✧CHAPTER 18✧

The Unfortunate Nose

As we slowly moved across the lake, the mist grew thicker until it was more like fog, and it became difficult to see where we were going. Eventually, all signs of the Pointing Finger were gone, and Tanaka had to rely on his sense of direction to keep us on course. I looked up at him, and couldn't help but think how strange this would have seemed if I had been able to look into the future a month or two ago.

Tanaka had grown very serious, his stern face a scowl, staring ahead with a concentrated gaze that made me think his eyes must be growing tired. The fog had dampened his hair and scraggly eyebrows. Without ever breaking his focus on what lay ahead, he slowly moved the long paddle in the water, switching between the sides of the raft, taking a couple of steps each time to span the wide raft.

The fog created an eerie silence, and the splashy sound of Tanaka's oar going in and out of the water echoed slightly. I began to worry that we were heading off course.

The sound of my sneeze exploded in the strange silence.

No one seemed to notice except Hood, who turned in my direction.

"Kaze ohiku," said Miyoko without a glance. A memory rushed into my head.

It was like that phrase again, the one I had heard back

on the train, the one that had to be the Japanese version of "bless you." That confirmed it. I had definitely sneezed back on the train, right before I lost the power of The Shield. It was just so hard to believe, so silly, but it had to be true. The act of sneezing is what turned The Shield on and off. But then, where was—

Something whipped past in the air above us, causing a disturbance in the fog. It made the same swooshing sound I'd heard in the woods by the river.

I knew what it had to be.

The Sounding Rod.

The only thing I didn't understand was why it wasn't making that awful noise.

"Miyoko, throw something at me, anything," I said.

"What? Why—"

"Just do it! I'll explain in a minute. Take out a flashlight or something and throw it at me like you want to hurt me. I just want to make sure The Shield works." I said this even though I had an almost certain feeling that it wouldn't. But, I knew she wouldn't throw it hard if she suspected anything.

She reached into her bag and pulled out a compass.

"Throw it as hard as you can," I urged her.

She pulled back, like a major leaguer, then heaved it straight for my face.

It whacked me in the nose, making me fall back into the arms of Hood. I had thought I'd be able to turn my head at least, but it came too fast. It hurt something awful.

Hood helped me back to a sitting position, and patted me on the back. As I rubbed my nose, willing the pain away, I thought that maybe our old Hood was finally back in true form, showing his unique sense of humor.

"That hurt," I said, very needlessly.

"What, what happened?" Miyoko asked. "Why did The Shield not protect you?" It was the first time I'd seen Miyoko look so concerned, including our little run from the mudslide.

"Well, I don't know exactly. It'll sound completely crazy to you guys."

Miyoko raised her eyebrows at me, then said, "Jimmy, I have a friend over there who won't let anyone see his face, travels through a red ring, and has paint coming out of his finger. Try me."

"Yeah, I see your point. Well, before I met up with Hood over there, my family was attacked by a bunch of men on motorcycles."

"The Bosu Zoku," Tanaka chimed in.

"You know them?" I asked.

"Yes, we know them," Miyoko explained. "They are all over Japan—they are the motorcycle gangs that try to disturb the peace and cause all kinds of trouble."

"They're that big? All over Japan, like the mafia?"

"No, no, that would be the Yakuza, our word for mafia. The Bosu Zoku are not organized. They are just a bunch of independently run gangs scattered throughout the country."

"Well, then, it must have just been a local gang that has been overrun by the Shadow Ka. We'd sure hoped they'd all been sucked out of people's minds when I blocked the Black Curtain, but I can't see how those people could have been anything but Shadow Ka. Their leader, Kenji, seemed to know everything, and he had the Sounding Rod, which is obviously not of this world."

"What do you mean?" asked Miyoko. "Look at the Hooded One. Do you think he is a Shadow Ka? Are you a Shadow Ka? You both have special powers, but you're both of this world. Maybe they are another group formed here on earth, just like us, except they're on the side of the Stompers and Shadow Ka. By the way, what is the Sounding Rod?"

"It's this weird black stick that can melt into a liquid and then re-form, so that it can go anywhere it wants. Kenji set it to following us, and said that I am the only person that can set it off. At the time, I didn't know what 'set it off' meant. When my family and I were on a train, it suddenly formed into this weird shaped cone, and let off a horrendous sound that made us all cover our ears. It made me lose The Shield, which is why Kenji and the Bosu Zoku were able to capture my family."

I went on to tell them the entire story in more detail, all the way up to following the clues left by Hood to find him in the house. Then I knew I had to lay my theory on them.

"Anyway, I think I might have figured out what sets off the Sounding Rod."

I gave them an uncertain look.

"Well, what is it?" Tanaka asked.

"Sneezing."

✧❩✧❩✧

"Sneezing." Miyoko didn't even ask it as a question, she just said it dully, like she was accusing me of being a smart-aleck.

"Sneezing?" Tanaka was perplexed. "Jimmy-san, you go crazy after mudslide?"

"No, I'm very serious, and I'm very not crazy. I've gone back in my mind, and every time the Sounding Rod either started or stopped, I'm almost certain that it coincided with me sneezing. I just can't figure out why the couple of times it has happened since the train I haven't been able to hear that same sound as before."

Tanaka and Miyoko were both in a state of deep thought, considering my whole story. I sat anxiously, their silence maddening, hoping that they believed me.

"Well," Miyoko finally chimed in, "I think I might know why."

"Really? What is it?" I was very interested.

"I'm in some advanced classes at my school, because I am abnormally intelligent."

She paused a second, letting that sink in. I think she was just joking around, but I wasn't certain. I didn't say anything, and just waited for her to go on.

"In one of my classes we've studied the properties of sound, waves and such. Sound can reach a point where it's so high, that humans can't hear it anymore. You've probably heard about dog whistles, where it's a very high-pitched sound that dogs can hear even though humans cannot."

"Hey, at the house where I met Hood, I could hear lots of dogs barking in the distance! I bet you're right! But why would it have changed after that first time on the train?"

"Well, if the sound is within a confined space, like the train, then it can bounce off whatever is holding it in, and those vibrations can make their own sound. Trains are made of metal, so maybe the horrible sound you heard was the violent reaction of the metal to the powerful waves emitting from the Sounding Rod. Also, sound waves can break glass, which would explain the broken windows at the house and on the train."

"Hmmm, that sounds like a pretty dang good explanation. You really are smart, Miyoko. I thought you'd be more like your dad."

Tanaka made a surprised grunting noise, like he wasn't quite sure he had heard me right.

I continued. "You know, I also wonder why it's hiding from me now. I haven't seen it as much since the train, although I think I've heard it flying by in the air above me a couple of times."

"Maybe it has its own brain. The first time, it wanted to make sure you understood its power, but now it's trying to have the element of surprise on its side, hoping you would not be able to figure out exactly when you lost The Shield, so that it would be harder for you to figure out the thing about the sneezing."

At that one moment, I was certain Miyoko was the smartest person alive. Well, at least the smartest fourteen-year-old alive, anyway.

"Wow," I said, "That's some deep stuff. But heck, it makes perfect sense to me. Doesn't help me get The Shield back, though. I need some sneezing powder for that. Which, by the way, leads to another question. Why in the world would a sneeze control that thing? Does that fit into your laws of physics too?"

"I can't explain that one. I don't know if the Sounding Rod is from this world, and it may have its own rules. But yeah, you're right. We need you to sneeze, and then never sneeze again. Simple, right?"

I was just about to reply when the raft slammed into something, throwing all of us forward. Miyoko had been standing, and fell on top of me, banging my head with her elbow. If I'd had The Shield, she would have been thrown into the water. Hood and Tanaka would have fallen into the water as well, except something stopped their forward progress, which they both hit hard with their heads.

I didn't realize that Tanaka had been that blinded by the fog.

We had arrived at the Pointing Finger.

✧CHAPTER 19✧
Ole Betsy's Strange Cousin

It was absolutely huge.

The Pointing Finger was as wide across as a big house, its rock glimmering a dark, shiny black. There was no shoreline, no gradual slope from the Finger down into the water. The towering pillar shot from the lake, straight up into the sky. We all followed its course with our eyes, looking at it go up and up and up, finally disappearing into the fog. From the shoreline where we'd first set off on the raft, it had not seemed so massive.

It was like an ancient castle tower, carved from black glass and smoothed out with dragon flame. Once again, I felt like I was in hobbit land. I half expected a wizard to open a secret door and invite us in for cakes.

As we gawked at this unbelievable structure, one thing became immediately clear.

There was no way we could climb this smooth tree of glass.

✧☽✧☽✧

"Jimmy-san," Tanaka joked. "Why you not pay attention, my friend? We could be killed crashing into big rock like that!"

He and Hood had regained their balance as well as their composure, and Miyoko and I untangled ourselves from

110

each other. We quickly put distance between us, feeling a little uncomfortable at having suddenly been so close. She gave me goose bumps again, and I still couldn't tell if that was a good thing or a bad thing.

"You need to sneeze, Jimmy, so we don't have to go through that again."

As if she had said a magic word, a sneeze exploded from my nose, and Tanaka bellowed as he wiped something off of his face. I was embarrassed, even though it was funny.

Miyoko threw a coin at me. I wasn't surprised when it bounded away from me only to hit Tanaka in the head. He was livid, although his slight smile showed it was feigned. Miyoko spoke through her laugh.

"Wow, that was quick. Now don't sneeze again."

"Jimmy-san, you much trouble. I might make you marry my daughter for punishment!"

"Very funny, Mr. Tanaka," I said back to him. "Now what do we do? I don't think my hands are sticky enough for me to climb that slippery rock."

"Ah, Mr. America, you need to trust Mr. Tanaka. You just watch, and maybe keep quiet, *neh*?" He said it with his patented smile.

He dipped the long oar back into the water. After banging into the black pillar, the raft had already drifted about ten feet from it. The creeping fog continued to fill the air all around us, as did the hanging silence, only broken by the hollow sound of our voices and the water lapping against the raft and paddle.

Tanaka steered us around the Finger, heading for the opposite side. We all stood with our eyes riveted to the black rock as we rounded it, waiting for whatever Tanaka was looking for. The fog made it hard to see, but we strained our eyes anyway.

Soon Tanaka pulled up his paddle and set its end on the raft. He leaned against it.

"So," he said. "You see it, Jimmy-san?"

"Yeah," was all I could manage.

The fog had cleared slightly from the side of the Finger, just enough to reveal some amazing structures protruding from the rock. Starting from the water and going all the way up, as far as we could see before being swallowed in the fog above, rods of black rock stuck out from the Pointing Finger in random fashion, pointing this way and that, scattered all about, with two or three feet between each one. My first thought was that it looked like a huge tree that had all of its branches sawed off about four feet from the trunk. The width of the area of branches was about fifteen feet across, continuing all the way up the Finger, and they were made of the same material as the pillar they protruded from, black and shiny.

Tanaka looked at me, seeing my amazement, and gave me a wink, hardly discernible under his enormous eyebrow.

"Ready to climb?" he asked.

"Mr. Tanaka, what would you say this pillar and all of those things sticking out of it remind you of?"

"Ah, a tree, *neh*?"

"That's right. And you're looking at the best dang tree-climber that ever walked the earth."

My statement seemed to surprise them, and they stared at me as I walked up to the edge of the raft and leaned out to grab one of the branches of rock. The excitement of climbing again filled me, and for one moment I forgot about all our troubles.

"Ganbarrrrro!" I yelled in my best Tanaka fashion, and pulled myself onto the wall of branches.

My companions followed, Tanaka's laugh piercing the foggy air.

✧❭✧❭✧

The black branches were perfectly spaced apart, the most ideal climbing tree I'd ever seen. This was the kind of tree I'd searched for my whole life, the kind of tree a four-teen-year-old dreamed about—even better than Ole Betsy back home. Of course, it wasn't a tree, but that was beside the point.

We started at a fast pace, moving from branch to branch, scaling the Finger like a team of lumberjacks. Hood had the most difficulty. He kept feeling around for the branches, groping like he couldn't quite see well enough. I still hadn't figured out how he could see in the first place through the robe. Maybe the blackness of everything combined with the fog was throwing off his version of sight. His robe kept catching on the black sticks as well, making it all the more difficult.

"Hang in there, Mr. Hood!" I yelled down at him.

He stuck out his right arm and brought his forearm up, as if to show his flexed muscles, though we couldn't see a thing through all that robe. But it gave us a good laugh.

It seemed strange under the circumstances to be having so much fun, but I couldn't have cared less. I felt like a kid again, and it was great.

We climbed and we climbed. Soon, all we could see both above and below was fog. It was an eerie feeling, clamber-ing up the side of this black tower of rock, seemingly lost in a world of white mist. I felt like Jack on his way up the beanstalk. I just hoped a man-eating giant never entered our story.

Soon the fatigue settled in, and the fun turned into

major labor. I began to believe the Pointing Finger went all the way to the moon. My arms and legs ached, and sweat poured down my face, despite the cool air. Miyoko and Tanaka seemed to be just fine, climbing with no effort whatsoever. Determined to keep my word that I was the best climber in the world, I tried to hide my fading strength, and kept moving along.

But it was getting harder and harder for Hood. Several times, we had to slow down or stop so that he could catch up. I feared he would slip and fall, and wondered if someone should climb underneath him. I almost voiced my thought when a whooping cry from Tanaka cut me short.

I looked up. The top was in sight.

And so was the woman standing there.

✧CHAPTER 20✧

A Very Strange Woman

My heart skipped a beat, and I nearly lost my grip. No one had ever mentioned that a person would be waiting for us at the top of the Finger. Her features were blurred in the misty air, but her form stood rigid, hands on her hips, looking down at us. The others did not appear alarmed, so I took a breath of relief and asked Miyoko about the woman.

"She is one of us," was her reply. "Her name is Rayna."

Miyoko didn't say another word and continued her climb.

I looked down at Hood, and asked him if he was okay. He nodded his huge, hooded head and reached for the next branch.

We scrambled up the last few spikes and climbed onto the top of the Finger. A wide pathway encircled the top, made from the same shiny black material. In the center was a vast, gaping hole. I carefully walked to the edge of the hole and glanced down.

A blast of warm air hit my face, and my head began to swim. It was deep, very deep. A red glow, very faint, came from somewhere at the bottom, slightly illuminating the inside of the massive, black shaft of metallic stone. Then I noticed something odd in the middle of the hole.

It was a . . . slide.

✧ ☽ ✧ ☽ ✧

Starting straight across from me, going from the outer circular path leading to the very center of the shaft, was a flat, smooth extension of the black rock. It then shot downwards in a tight spiral, winding and winding like a curlyque French fry for as far down as I could see in the red light. The entire structure was one piece, and stood like another tower within the one we had just ascended. It looked for all the world like a kid's wildest dream come true. A slide for the ages.

I glanced over at the woman named Rayna, still standing firm with her hands on her hips, and got a good look at her for the first time. She had long, wavy brown hair, and a face that would make even the most courageous man screech like a baby and run away.

Rayna was flat-out ugly.

Hideous was a better word. Her face bore all kinds of pocks and scars, and her nose was the size of a small mountain. One of her ears stuck out through her hair, the other seemed withered, almost hidden from sight. One of her eyes was missing, leaving a mass of bulbous scar tissue. She was dressed from head to toe in leather, dyed the bright green of lime pie. I felt like I was looking at some kind of deranged comic book hero.

She noticed the look of wonder on my face.

"Jimmy Fincher," she said, her voice gruff, matching her appearance. "It's okay to stare the first time. After that, try to refrain. I am of the Alliance. We are the humble and the neglected. We are here to help you, so please return our respect."

I didn't quite know how to respond.

"Of . . . of course," I somehow got out.

She walked along the path, stopping within a few feet of me.

"There are two things about me that you will find quite fascinating, Jimmy. Two amazing facts. One I will tell you now, the other you must figure out for yourself."

Rayna then told me her story.

✧CHAPTER 21✧

Stories and Slides

Rayna was from America, but had moved to Japan with her parents when she was a child. Both parents had been killed in a train wreck, and Rayna was left on the streets. Years of hard living left her in the state she was in, battered and weathered. But she'd had a special ability, and it eventually led her to the Alliance.

Rayna's gift was something that seemed impossible to me. Not because it was weird or unusual or magical—that sort of thing had become second nature in my life. Her gift was unbelievable because it had to do with the future.

She could do amazing things with photographs.

When Rayna touches a photo, it *changes*. It becomes a window to the future, slowly alternating between many possible outcomes for whoever is in the picture. No outcome is certain or set in stone. The alternating pictures are merely *possibilities.*

For years, Rayna wondered how such a talent could be of any use. She soon came to the conclusion that by seeing what *may* happen, one can work towards those things that they *want* to happen.

Something in my mind clicked. The horror of those pictures I saw at the house where I met Hood came slamming back into my head. The blank faces of my family, appearing dead, our bodies lying on stone beds, in a dark, gray world.

Joseph had told me that's what happens when the

Stompers come. That's what lay in my future. The mystery of it and the terror of it were equally mind-numbing.

"You did this to some pictures of my family, didn't you?" I asked. "I saw them in the house by the river, where I met Hood."

I looked over at him, and he shrunk away, lowering his head and refusing to answer.

"Yes," Rayna replied, "I had pictures of your family, and I touched them with my ability. We needed to know what might lie in your future, so we would know what we could do to either help or hinder. I sent them with The Hooded One as a way to convince you that we are your friends. It sounds like you were unlucky enough to see something that was not pleasant. We should have been more careful."

"But where did you get a picture of us?"

"From your father, of course."

"My dad? You know my dad?"

"There is a lot about me that will surprise you, Jimmy. But we've talked long enough. We need to descend into the Finger—time is running short."

"But—"

Miyoko cut me off. "Rayna is correct. Let's go. You'll have plenty of time to reminisce after we save the world."

Frustrated, I followed the others as they walked around the circular path to the other side of the Finger, where the black extension leading to the strange slide began. Hood shuffled along behind me. Miyoko, Tanaka, and Rayna stopped next to the protruding piece of rock, and looked out towards the curly-que slide.

A question had been burning in my mind since I'd first looked at the thing, and I finally voiced it.

"It looks like a lot of fun, but how in the world do we get back up?"

"Oh, mister Jimmy-san," Tanaka answered, "you have much to learn about our world. This no ordinary stone path. This a magic path, and coming up is better than going down! You wait and see, my friend."

With that, and a hackling laugh, Tanaka walked out onto the extension towards the middle and sat down, his legs pointing down in the direction of the descending slide. He looked back at me with his bad-toothed grin.

"Jimmy-san, don't be scared. Tanaka will catch you at the bottom."

He pushed off with his hands and shot down the slide. It appeared to be greased or something the way he flew. Winding around and around, he disappeared into the darkness below, his screams of delight slowly fading the further he went.

✧⟫✧⟫✧

"Hooded One," Rayna called out, "you are next."

Hood shook his head and took a step backwards.

"What is wrong with you?" Rayna asked. "You've done this before, now come on!"

She walked over to him and gently grabbed his arm. Hood whipped it away from her, and for a second I thought he would hit her. Something was terribly wrong with this guy. He was so obviously shaken from whatever had happened to him—I just wished he'd talk—or write—to us about it.

He recovered his composure and waved his hand as an apology. He walked carefully out to the slide and sat down. Then, with his arms shaking, he pushed off and flew down the slide, his ugly robed form appearing and disappearing as he wound his way to the bottom.

Miyoko was next. She gave me a wink, and without any

hesitation whatsoever, ran across the path and jumped feet forward onto the slide, shooting downward even faster than the other two.

Rayna put her hand on my shoulder.

"I will go last. Don't be afraid. Tanaka is a silly man, but he wasn't lying. This black, winding path is indeed very mysterious and powerful. It will not let you fall, and will deliver you safely to the bottom. And just you wait until we come back up—that will be something you'll never forget. Now, go. You will be protected."

With a gentle push, she set me off towards the path. I was more fascinated than I was scared. At the moment, I knew I had The Shield, and that I could simply jump to the bottom if I really wanted to. But I still didn't quite love that sensation of falling through the air and then bouncing around like a ping-pong ball, so I chose the slide.

As I walked across the extension towards the middle, I looked over the edge on both sides of me. There appeared to be nothing at all supporting the entire structure except this one line of rock attached to the circular path on top of the Finger. The winding slide went down and down and down, until it finally disappeared into that faint red glow. I suddenly realized that the shaft inside the Finger was much, much deeper than what we had just climbed to get to this point. Shield or no Shield, I was finally scared.

I sat down on the edge of where it started to turn into the downward slide, and took a deep breath. I'd always loved roller coasters, but this was beyond anything I'd ever done. I also remembered that rides at the amusement parks that went in circles always made me sick. Well, there wasn't much choice, so I told myself to quit thinking and pushed off.

The black rock was slick, and my body rocketed toward

the ground faster than any roller coaster I'd ever been on. Round and round, wind rushing past me, I flew down the slide. It was fun until my stomach started to disagree with the experience.

As I got sicker and sicker, I could sense the red glow intensifying, but soon couldn't take it anymore. I closed my eyes, and prayed for it to hurry up and end.

It went on and on and on, circling, spinning, flying down the shaft of the Finger. After a while, the surface of the slide grew less slick, and my speed slowed somehow. Then the faint sound of Tanaka came rolling up from below, and before long, I shot off the slide into the arms of the laughing Japanese man, knocking him to the ground.

Nauseous to the core, I then threw up on him.

For the first time since I'd met him, I saw Tanaka frown.

✧CHAPTER 22✧

The Glowing Cavern

Before I could recover and sit up, I was kicked in the back of the head by a flying woman named Rayna, The Shield making her bounce up and over me. It surprised me more than it hurt her, and for some strange reason we all started laughing. Even stinky, frowning Tanaka finally broke a smile as he did his best to wipe the sludge off of his clothes.

Still giggling for no particular reason, I slowly stood and took in my surroundings.

We were in an enormous cavern, carved out of brown stone, very different from the black material of the Finger and slide. The cavern went in all directions for hundreds and hundreds of feet, in some places even extending so far that I couldn't see where it ended. The ceiling of the cavern was at least a few hundred feet above us as well. It was just plain huge.

Then I noticed the source of the red glow.

Dotted here and there throughout the floor of the cave were pools of hot, simmering lava. As if brought on by the sight, I realized how incredibly hot it was in that place. A slight draft was flowing through the air, and it was very warm. I touched my face and pulled away a hand wet with sweat.

I remembered the stupid story I used to tell my friends about how my grandpa had died in a volcano, one of the worst stories ever concocted by a dad trying to explain a death to his kid. Well, who would've thought it would come back to haunt me?

I was smack dab in the middle of a bona fide volcano. I couldn't help but wonder when the last time was that this thing erupted.

Then I saw the book.

✧ ☽ ✧ ☽ ✧

About a hundred feet from the bottom of the slide, next to the closest cave wall, was a tall block of stone, the top of it slanted downward slightly to the side facing us. On that stone rested a large, closed book. I couldn't make out many details, but I had no doubt that it had to be the book. The Book. An eerie feeling came over me, realizing that my dad had once been in this place, and had looked at that very book.

I stepped towards it.

"Wait!"

Rayna's voice boomed in the vast cave, echoing off the walls like someone introducing a speaker at a school assembly. I looked back at her.

"Before you do this, you may want to take a minute and get yourself under control. You will only have one shot at this, and you must not fail."

"One shot?" I asked, puzzled. "What do you mean, one shot? What am I taking a shot at?"

"Have you already forgotten the riddle?" Miyoko answered for Rayna.

"The riddle? Oh yeah, the one about the fire and ice. No, I hadn't forgotten, I guess. I just didn't really understand what it would mean or what I would have to do about it." I paused and took a deep breath. "I guess I haven't really thought about anything except finding the book up until now. What am I supposed to do? I thought I would read the book and somehow I would then have the Second Gift."

"Surely, you have learned by now that the Givers do not work that way," Rayna replied. "To them, everything is a test. One must prove themselves worthy before they receive their reward. Why in the world do you think your dad had to come to Japan to get a key that opens a door way back in Georgia? Nothing in this battle will ever be easy. You must pass certain tests to prove that you are the one who will bear the Gifts in the battle against the Stompers."

"I guess I figured I'd already proven myself. Plus, isn't it true that now that I've received the First Gift, no one else can receive the others?"

"Yes," Rayna said, "but that doesn't change anything. Just because you have passed one test, and have been set on this path, does not mean that your need for growth has lessened. If anything, that need has only grown more urgent. You have a lot to learn, and a lot to receive before you will be able to defeat the Stompers. Remember, you have no idea or concept of what the Stompers really are. It's not like you're going to battle a bunch of monsters or robots or aliens. The Stompers are something quite different."

"Why can't someone just tell me what they are, then?"

Miyoko replied this time. "Two reasons. One, none of us truly even know that much about them. Only the Givers do. And two, that is also part of your growth process. You will not be able to defeat them unless you have come to understand them for yourself."

Filled with frustration, I just couldn't understand. I felt so blind to the purpose of everything, I wondered how in the world I could keep going. I felt that hopeless feeling coming back, and I wanted to cry and give up. But something, deep inside of me, stood firm, and I snapped myself out of it.

"Okay, what do I need to do?"

This time, Tanaka wanted to answer. He walked up to me, and whipped out his usual smile.

"Jimmy-san, you must go to the book. We brought you here, we told you the riddle. That is all we can do." He grabbed my hand into both of his, and then continued, "We are your deepest friends. We are here for you. You will come back. Go, now."

Tanaka let go of my hand, and gestured towards the stone altar and the book. I looked around at everyone else, saw their supportive eyes and willful expressions, and built up my resolve. It was time to do some reading. I turned and began walking towards the stone pillar.

I had just taken my third step when Hood went insane.

I would never make it to the book.

✧CHAPTER 23✧

The Hood Taken Off

I heard footsteps pounding the pavement behind me, and I turned around just in time to see Hood jump into the air in front of me and sail over my head. I jerked around towards the book in time to see him land. Dazed at his leaping abilities, I froze, looking at him. He turned and slowly walked up to me until he was inches from my face. I took a step back, uncomfortable with his strange behavior.

Hood reached into the deep folds of his robe, and pulled out a clenched fist of something that he kept hidden. He slowly raised his hand until it was right in front of my face. Every instinct of my body told me to run, that Hood had gone nuts and that he was going to hurt me. But my trust in him proved greater, and I stood my ground.

Then everything happened in a maddened rush.

Hood flipped his hand open, and a swarm of flying dust filled the air around me. The Shield kicked into gear, repelling the dust outwards like a big bubble, but it had been too late. My trust in Hood overcame the protective power of The Shield. Just enough of the strange dust flew into my nose, and I let out a huge sneeze.

From somewhere above us, the Sounding Rod swooped down until it was just a few feet above me. That familiar cone formed, and then its soundless cry blasted into the air, its vibration felt in my bones despite the lack of sound.

Just like that, The Shield was gone.

✧)✧)✧

Confused, I stared at Hood, wondering what had over-come him, and why he would want my protection to disap-pear. A great tremor of fear boiled up inside me. Something was terribly wrong.

A chuckling sneer suddenly filled the air around us. After a brief moment of confusion, I realized the sound was coming from Hood. Miyoko, Rayna, and Tanaka came closer, all of us staring at our hooded companion with dis-belief. None of us had ever heard any kind of sound come from underneath that hood before.

Then, calmly, Hood reached up with his hands and slid the hood over his head. It fell over and settled onto his back.

Even as the sound of Miyoko's screams filled the cavern, I could only stand frozen, staring with unbelieving eyes at the person who stood before me.

With a wicked sneer and frightful eyes that were deep black, he stared back, and the nightmares of past days invaded my mind.

It was him.

Custer Bleak, the leader of the Union of Knights, the leader of the Shadow Ka on our world.

The one man on the planet who completely terrified me.

Raspy.

✧)✧)✧

The first person able to speak was Rayna.

"What have you done with the Hooded One?" she screamed at Raspy.

"He is tied to a tree, as if it really matters," he replied in that distinct voice, like a man with a frog in his throat, sending chills through my whole body. "As you know, I could not kill him, but his scaly, weak body could do nothing to stop me from tying him up. However, that is a matter which should be far down on your list of things to worry about."

Raspy took a step closer to me, his black eyes riveted on mine the entire time. I looked into his voided eyes, wondering what was happening. His eyes had not been like that the last time I saw him, during that intense hurricane of destruction in the Blackness.

He sensed my question.

"Jimmy, my boy," he said, tipping his head to one side and smiling without humor, "what strange things you have seen in the last few weeks. You must continue to think that you've seen it all, yet more and more comes at you. Believe me when I say, I feel sorry for you. I feel sorry for every person on this tired and sad world of yours. I feel excitement for the day when the Stompers will relieve you from this drudgery of an existence." He rubbed his ancient, gnarled hands together. "For the day they free your minds forever."

As usual, I had no idea what Raspy was talking about. I could only stare at those eyes, and could think of nothing to say. My insides hurt with anguish.

"We are morphing, Jimmy. We are evolving. Your blocking of the Black Curtain was brave, my boy, but in the end, a waste. There are enough of us to reach the next stage. We will soon be ready. But you, I'm afraid, are a nuisance that we still need to dispose of, just as any king would want the last rat banished from his castle.

"How strange, isn't it, about your Shield? So powerful,

so dominating, so very scary. But you yourself keep making it go away. It's a shame to have to witness such sad irony, all because of that special gift you gave Mayor Duck so long ago."

Intense curiosity finally overcame my inability to speak.

"What do you mean?"

"The tree, boy, don't you remember?" he asked in his scratchy voice. "The day it all started, the day you saw Mayor Duck and . . ." He looked behind me with a smile, as if deep in thought. "That day, Jimmy. You gave Duck a most precious gift. Your sneeze."

"Do the Shadow Ka ever learn to just speak and quit beating around the bush? What are you talking about?"

"Getting braver and braver, aren't we?" he continued. "We found a glitch in The Shield, a small one, a very small one. The Sounding Rod. It's unearthly song would break your barrier, but it had to have a catalyst, a natural one. It had to be from you. We couldn't let it be a word or something that you could easily control once you learned of it. Finally, it was a precious memory from Duck that solved everything. Your sneeze. It has a distinct sound to it, Jimmy, has anyone every told you that?"

I didn't answer. I was only getting sicker to my stomach the more he spoke. I started thinking about sneezing, and tried my hardest to make myself do it. It was pointless.

"It worked beautifully. Duck shared his memory with us, and we instilled it into the Sounding Rod. Ah, the sharing of our minds, what a beautiful thing, boy. You should covet such a gift. It makes The Four so trivial. So worthless. You should hide in a hole until the day the Stompers come.

"Anyway, you make me ramble, boy! Kenji and his men

planned it all so perfectly on the train, planting the dust and waiting for the right moment. They wanted your family as collateral but let you go, knowing that this pitiful Alliance would find you and lead you here. Now, finally, I can end everything, and the last obstacle in our path will be removed."

Raspy leapt into the air, ignoring gravity, and hovered there for just a second, and then came back down.

"Ah, it is happening so fast, it feels so wonderful," he said into the air, no longer talking to us, his madness made evident.

He turned his back to us, then leapt into the air again, shooting forward towards the stone altar and the book. Fear ripped me out of my coma-like state and I ran forward, afraid of his intent. I had no Shield, but I could not sit and watch him as he . . .

It was too late.

With almost no effort, and with even less care, Raspy picked up the dusty book from its perch and tossed it into the closest lava pool.

I stopped in my tracks, eyes wide, heart sinking, and stared as the book disappeared into the impossibly hot liquid, burning as it went, sinking in a sizzle of flame.

The Book.

The Book for which I'd come all the way to Japan.

The Book that was to deliver the remaining Gifts to me.

The Book.

It was gone.

✧CHAPTER 24✧

Raspy Flies

I fell to the ground, my knees too weak from the shock of what Raspy had just done. I stared at the pool of lava, hoping against all reason that somehow it would come sailing out of the hot bubbles and smack Raspy on the head, knocking him into the steaming pool.

Despair cankered my heart.

"It's gone, Jimmy. Without the other Gifts, there is nothing you can do now." Raspy smiled an awful grin. "The Four Gifts' purposes must work as a whole, or do nothing. Now, you are without even your precious Shield. It is tempting to leave you for the wonder of the Stompers when they come, but I have had enough of you. Time to die."

Raspy leapt at me with the speed of lightning.

Parts of his body blurred into blackness, like living shadow, and before I could tell what was what, something big and hard whacked me in the head. It sent me reeling. I tumbled over and over, coming to a stop right next to a pool of lava.

Hurting, I pinned my eyes on Raspy and caught a glimpse of swirling blackness around his arms, like mini-tornadoes of dark dust. They disappeared, leaving his normal arms in their place. I had no idea what I'd just seen.

Raspy leapt again, intent on one more attack to end it all. Looking on with little strength to fight back, I readied myself for an attempt to kick him into the lava when he came down on top of me. It would never happen.

Rayna and Miyoko attacked Raspy from two directions, stopping him short. Just a few feet from where I sat, they pummeled him from both sides, like some kind of tag-team wrestling move. Their attack was perfectly timed and fierce, and Raspy collapsed beneath them. Tanaka came from behind, propelled by rage, and jumped into the air, coming down with his legs aimed at Raspy's face.

There was a blur of darkness and a swirling of shadow, and Raspy was gone before Tanaka landed. Our eyes shot to a place behind Tanaka where Raspy had come to a stop. He jumped into the air and flew over towards the black slide and the shaft of the Pointing Finger.

Black shapes trailed him, and for a second I was sure he had grown wings, but the shapes were gone as soon as I noticed them.

He landed, and turned towards us again.

"It matters not. You will not receive the Gifts, and you will not leave this place."

He reached his hands into the folds of his robe and pulled out what looked like two apples.

"A toy of your people," he yelled, "a toy of your making! We find them useful."

Raspy then pulled the stem off the apples and threw them at the base of the slide. The clanking as they bounced and rolled to a stop underneath the exit of the slide revealed that the objects were most definitely not apples.

They were hand-grenades.

With a wicked laugh, Raspy then shot upwards into the shaft of the Finger, gone before we knew it, his laugh trailing away as he rocketed skywards. We could only wonder in horror at these new powers he was starting to show in our world.

My companions understood as well as I what Raspy had done.

We collapsed to the ground and held our hands over our ears.

The boom of the exploding grenades rocked the air, but it was nothing compared to the crashing sound of black stone collapsing from above.

✧◗✧◗✧

The crashing seemed to go on forever. Our terror made us cower on the ground and shake with fright. The splitting and cracking of the slide collapsing on itself was deafening, and we were sure it would never end until the whole Finger collapsed.

We cowered, hands pinned to our heads in a meager effort to protect our ears, and endured the thunderous collapse of our only hope for escape.

It finally ended, and black dust swirled from the opening of the shaft, a few more faint sounds of settling stone travelling with it.

We coughed and wheezed and spit and then gathered ourselves together, looking as one towards the opening.

"What we do now?" Tanaka asked no one in particular.

"Let's have a look," answered Rayna.

We waited until the dust had mostly settled, then walked over to the big pile of shiny black rubble. It was a mess, pieces of stone lying on top of each other all over the place. I looked up, and could just make out something in the middle of the shaft. Miyoko gasped.

"It didn't destroy the whole thing!" she proclaimed, her voice echoing eerily up the long stone shaft of the pillar. She was right. We all agreed that we could just make out where the slide had broken off, the remainder winding its way up the Finger to the very top.

Still hurting, but feeling a little better, I asked, "How in the world can that small strip of rock at the top support it now that it's not attached at the bottom?"

"Because it's special," was Rayna's answer.

"What you really mean is that you don't know," I said back to her.

"You would be right," she said with a scowl, and walked back into the massive cavern.

We followed her, and sat in a circle on the ground, looking at each other, waiting for some brilliant ideas.

"Well," Rayna finally said, "it doesn't really matter that the whole thing didn't collapse, because there's no way to get to where it starts up again. Plus, the insides of the Finger are as smooth as glass, and there is no chance of climbing it. And, I know of no other way out. Any ideas?"

Silence was her only answer.

That's when I saw the door.

A wooden door, one that looked very familiar.

✧CHAPTER 25✧

A Door in the Stone

There is no way we could've missed it earlier. It was in the wall right beside the stone altar where the book had been lying. It was made of a dark wood, and looked exactly like the one at the end of the tunnel below the door in the woods near my home—the one that led to the First Gift. It had the same curved iron handle, with both ends attached to the wood.

When I pointed out the door to the others, they became animated.

"That was definitely not there before," said Miyoko.

"I didn't notice it either," said Rayna. "It must've appeared when the book was destroyed."

"It looks just like the door I opened when I first met the Givers, when I received the First Gift."

"Jimmy-san," yelled Tanaka, "you must open it! Open it!"

The others agreed.

"Maybe there is still hope after all," said Rayna. "That door is meant to be opened. We all know who must do it."

The three of them looked at me, and I couldn't disagree.

"Okay, you're right. It just seems so weird that it just appeared like that."

"Jimmy," said Rayna, "we just saw a lunatic fly off into the sky. I wouldn't worry about things seeming strange.

We will wait for you." Like they were going to go anywhere anyway.

I got up and walked over to the wall with the door in it. As I approached the stone altar near the wall, I noticed that there was a small square cut into the top of it. I went up to it and traced my finger around it.

"It looks like maybe there was a trigger or something that was set off when Raspy, I mean Custer, lifted the book from the altar."

They walked over and inspected it themselves.

"Looks like our shadow friend didn't quite look beyond the tip of his nose," said Miyoko. "He may have done exactly what was meant to happen, although I can't imagine the book was supposed to be destroyed."

"Well," I said, "whatever happened, this door is begging for me to come on in. I feel good about it since it looks so similar to the door that led me to the First Gift. Wish me luck."

It seemed like a stupid thing to say, but I couldn't think of anything else. I walked over to the door, paused, grabbed the long handle, then pulled.

It swung open effortlessly, but all I could see inside was darkness. After one last look at my friends of the Alliance, I stepped through, and let the door close behind me.

It made no sound.

✧⟩✧⟩✧

The instant the door shut completely, the room lit up with a brilliant flare. It was blinding, and I put my hands over my eyes. I turned and squinted towards the door I'd just walked through.

It was gone.

All around me was . . . nothing. Nothing but a brilliant

white light. My eyes began to adjust.

I was in the very center of a large, round room made completely of white marble—floor, walls, and ceiling. A light seemed to shine through the marble, making the room almost unbearably bright. To my right, about twenty feet away and built into the round, marble wall was a big archway, almost twice as tall as me, apparently an exit from the room. But it was completely blocked in with another wall of black marble, indented slightly past the archway.

I looked over to my left, directly opposite from the blocked exit. There, in the wall, was another exit, an exact copy of the one I'd just been studying. The same white marble archway, blocked in by a wall of black marble. But this one had something on the floor right in front of it.

It was a small wooden table, on which a book rested, similar to the one Raspy had destroyed just moments before. My heart skipped a beat. Maybe this was the real book. I walked up to it and flipped through its pages. It had a very old feel to it, like something you'd find in an old, dusty antique shop. But all of the pages were empty.

Except one.

The very first page had six lines written on it. I had seen the words before.

enter the fire, turn to the cold
express your desire, you must be bold
the fire will kill you, there is no doubt
the Ice will fill you, the other way out
beware the rift, see it and die
steps be swift, do not turn the eye

The riddle of ice and fire.

✧⟩✧⟩✧

Too bad I had no idea what it meant. I concentrated on the words, forcing myself to memorize them even if I didn't understand their meaning. There was no doubt that the purpose of the riddle was critical, and I burned the words into my mind.

Then I noticed that lying next to the book was a big feather, it's long quill dirty with black ink at the end. An ancient pen, or pencil, or whatever they used to call it when they'd write by dipping those things in ink and then scratching them along their paper. A book, mostly blank, with a feather next to it. Things weren't clearing up very quickly.

Why couldn't the Givers be here? They'd been there for me for the First Gift, and I felt like I needed them more than ever. I had absolutely no clue as to what I should do.

The lights went out, sending my heart through my throat.

I was just about to panic and scream, when the lights came on, shining once again through the white marble walls, floor, and ceiling. Things had changed.

I was in the middle of the room again. The archways were now much further apart, the room ten times bigger. The black marble walls blocking the archways were gone. I stared in wonder at what was beyond the exits.

The archway to my left, the one that still held the table and book, now led into a wall of flame. Loud, crackling fire burned intensely, filling the entire archway. Flame licked and spit, like a huge bonfire, almost too bright to look at. I could feel the heat from where I was standing.

I looked at the other exit.

It was the opposite in every way. Misty swirls of air moved

up and down and across the opening, like the entrance to
a huge freezer. Icicles covered the curved top of the arch,
hanging down almost halfway to the floor, ending in sharp
points. Frost covered the remaining edges of the exit. It was
impossible to see beyond the mist at what lay beyond.

One doorway to a burning inferno. Another doorway
leading to an icy freezer. A table with a book and pen.

Again, I wondered what I should do, and nothing
came.

After several minutes, with no progress, I sat down on
the marble floor, and put my mind to work. The riddle was,
after all, a riddle, and I figured I'd better get busy trying to
solve the dumb thing.

It said I was supposed to enter the fire. By the looks of
it, I decided that would burn me up in no time. But then I
thought that maybe it was a test, and that it wouldn't actually hurt me. But no, the riddle made it very clear that the
fire would kill me. *No doubt*, it said. Obviously, the Givers
did not want me dead, yet they told me to go into the fire,
yet they told me it would definitely kill me. It didn't make
any sense!

I thought and I thought and I thought.

Enter the fire.

Enter the fire.

Enter the fire.

I thought about the word on a deeper level. It had to
have different meanings, because the obvious one, the definition that sounded like it wanted me to walk into the fire
and die, just couldn't be right. The only time I had ever
really come across the word "enter" was when I had used
a computer. The "enter" button was what you pushed to
"enter" something into the computer. To input something
into the computer.

Could it mean . . . ?

Why else would the fire door have the book and pen, and the ice door not?

They wanted me to *enter* "the fire," not go into the fire and die!

Excited, I walked up to the book on the table. I flinched at the intense heat pulsing through the archway. I picked up the quill pen, flipped open the book, and wrote the words "the fire" into the book.

Then, following the riddle's next words, I *turned* to the cold.

I swiveled my body around, putting my back to the fire, and looked towards the frozen archway on the other side of the chamber.

Suddenly, it seemed miles away. I could barely see it. The room had continued to grow to an enormous size. The marble floor stretched on and on, with the other door barely visible now, way in the distance.

And I noticed something coming towards me from that direction.

✦CHAPTER 26✦
The Desire

At first, it was a gray blur. Then it began to take the shape of many points of gray, flying towards me, coming faster and faster. My stomach turned.

The points reached the middle of the vast room. They were traveling at a blistering speed now and I finally realized what was coming.

Long, sharp, metal spears, hundreds of them. Light reflected off of their metallic shafts and points. Their tips were blades, and I could only assume that they were really sharp.

The metal spears flew faster and faster, all coming straight for me. Thoughts spun through my head, panic surged through my body. I only had seconds. Forcing myself to think, I thought of the riddle.

The spears were still coming.

The riddle, the riddle.

The spears were almost to me.

The riddle.

Express your desire, you must be bold.

The spears.

Only seconds away.

Express your desire.

The spears, coming fast, coming with tips of death.

You must be bold.

Express your . . . yes! At that precise moment, there was

only one desire in the world that mattered.

My voice boomed throughout the chamber.

"I DO NOT WANT . . ."

The spears, just feet away.

"TO BE KILLED . . ."

Inches.

"BY THE SPEARS!!!"

With a metallic whisper of air, the spears vanished, and all was silent.

They had disappeared an inch before they ripped into my body.

Seconds later, I reminded myself to breathe.

✧CHAPTER 27✧
The End of the Riddle

The vast chamber became deathly silent, my breathing the only sound. I looked around, expecting someone to pop out and congratulate me for not being killed by the spears. My mind was still working through the details. What purposes were being fulfilled by these tests, these riddles?

But it wasn't over yet.

The fire would kill me, which didn't seem like rocket science to figure out, and the Ice would fill me, the other way out. Well, there was only one other way out, the arched room across from me, its edges icy and cold.

Beware the rift, see it and die . . . what and where was a rift? And how could I avoid it if I didn't see it? My brain was starting to hurt.

Steps be swift, do not turn the eye. That could only mean one thing, and now two things were for sure. The icy door was my way out, and my feet needed to be swift about it.

Taking one last deep breath, I bolted across the room towards the other archway.

A sudden and violent cracking noise boomed and echoed throughout the white cavern, coming from behind me. Splitting rock and potent crunching noises exploded into the air. With a little shriek I ran faster. Every inch of my body screamed at me to turn and look at it, at the source of this dreadful noise, this thunderous danger that approached from behind. But the riddle was clear on one point.

See it and die . . . do not turn the eye. Over and over I told myself this as I ran, overloading every instinct that was telling me to turn my head and look.

I was halfway to the archway and the iciness behind it.

My feet pounded the white marble, arms swinging, body straining, head leaning forward, pushing myself faster and faster. The horrible fracturing of the rock behind me was getting closer and closer. I could sense the growing crevice, the *rift*, ripping through the ground, trying its best to catch my feet and send me to the depths of whatever waited below.

Closer, almost there.

Still fighting the instinct to look back, I ran on. The ground shook below me, felt looser. I faltered a bit, barely catching myself, knowing that one slip and the rift would be on me.

Only feet away.

The air filled with sounds of splintering rock. My feet and legs were ready to give up, my head wanted so badly to look, to look back at the rift.

With one last push, I took the last frantic steps and dove through the icy entrance, just underneath the hanging icicles. The storm of sounds ceased in an instant, and the world became very cold.

CHAPTER 28

A Gift of Ice

There was the brief sound of a soft hum. It was the same sound I'd heard when the door in the woods closed after descending the stone stairway back in Georgia. Quickly, I glanced behind me.

The large wooden door with the iron handle was back, closed tight.

I looked back into the room, and the cold hit me like a wall of icy water. The room was freezing, and there was a strong breeze blowing, icy snow slapping at my body, everything defying my senses of being inside a room. I could still see walls, completely covered in ice, but everything else felt like I was outside during a blizzard. With no Shield to protect me, I thought I'd be frozen dead pretty darn soon.

A shadow moved past my vision.

I jerked my head in that direction, and saw a figure, standing, obscured in the impossible snowstorm. Shivers flew up and down my body, this time from eerie fright, not the cold.

The figure moved towards me, slowly trudging back and forth. It was huddled in a mass of blankets and clothing, wrapped from head to toe.

The figure stopped two feet in front of me. Then it . . . he . . . spoke.

"Our ways cross again, my friend. Welcome."

With that, he reached up and pulled back his hood of

garments. An ancient, withered, and familiar face looked into my eyes.

Farmer.

✧ ☽ ✧ ☽ ✧

Shivering almost uncontrollably, I wasn't even that shocked. I could only think of being cold.

"How?" I asked. "The Black Curtain is blocked! How did you come here?"

"Jimmy!" he yelled back, trying to speak above the sounds of the wind and beating snow. "Do you really think there is a room of snow and ice in the middle of a volcano? It is you, my friend, who have come to me. These are special places where we meet! They have nothing to do with the Curtain or the Blackness. You have much to learn."

He leaned forward and cracked a smile with his purple, shivering lips.

"You are quite remarkable, young man. You have made it so far, yet there is so much more to see. Ah, bother! Come, I have something for you."

We stepped towards the middle of the frigid room and I asked him about the purpose of the riddle of ice and fire.

"Growth, Jimmy. Progression. Learning. Strength. Your path leads to something that you must be prepared for. It is for that reason we have set these trials in place. One day, you will understand, and you will know, and you will be thankful. Now, this bothersome noise is getting me cranky, so let's get on with it!"

Farmer reached into the layers of his clothing, and pulled out a small red box, which appeared to be made from polished wood. With a flick of his hands, the box opened on a hinge. The inside was cushioned with black velvet.

Lying on the velvet, right in the middle, was a piece of

ice. A crudely formed ice cube, frosted and misshapen.

I looked up into Farmer's eyes, my own full of questions.

"This is it, my boy. Take it."

"What is it?" I could hardly speak now, my body shaking. "Is it..."

"Of course it is. Take it."

The Second Gift.

It seemed so unreal. After all the journeying, after all the close calls, after all the adventures, here I was, in the middle of a blizzard, being offered a piece of ice. I had no doubts anymore—it was just so strange.

There, ready for the taking. The Second Gift.

With trembling hands, I reached out and grabbed the cube of ice. It sent a wintry chill down my arms and into my chest. I knew it would be cold, but it was really, really cold. It had the slight roughness that ice has when first brought into contact with something warm. It stuck to my fingers for a second, then grew slick as it melted. From my experience with Farmer under the door in the woods, I knew he wanted me to eat it, just like I had drunken the silvery liquid to obtain the First Gift.

I looked up at Farmer, and he nodded.

With trembling hands I brought it to my mouth, popped it in, and chewed it up, just like ice from a soda. It had no taste.

The blizzard disappeared, as did some of the surrounding ice and snow. The room was instantly warmer, although still chilly. Farmer took off his excess clothing, revealing a tattered old flannel shirt and dusty overalls.

"Good," he said, strangely cheerful. "You have just received a gift most precious, to go along with your other, of course. By the way, we are indeed sorry for the slight miscalculation on our part."

"Slight?" I asked.

"Jimmy," he replied, now in a much more somber voice. "Nothing is or can be perfect, for reasons you may come to understand. We placed the flaw of The Shield with full knowledge of its existence and risk. But the odds of the Ka discovering it . . . just mind-boggling. After all these eons, I can't believe we once again underestimated them. Oh well, it is solved. You will destroy the Sounding Rod, and they will never be able to duplicate their deed."

"Destroy it? How? That thing is indestructible."

"It is, you say? It is not, I say. Let's move on. Our time is short, as usual."

Farmer walked a few feet away and sat down, although I did not remember seeing a chair.

"Now," he said, "The Second Gift. It is extremely important, Jimmy. You will not know how much so for quite some time, but I assure you, it is vital to our cause. In the end, it will make or break our struggle against the evil forces that beset us."

He paused, lost in thought, before looking up.

"Jimmy, raise your right arm."

"We've been through this before," I answered back.

"Jimmy, raise your right arm. Please."

I did as he asked.

"Jimmy, raise your other arm."

I did.

"Just as easily as you have done this, and just as easily as you now call upon The Shield, you can now call upon a new and formidable power. The Ice has filled you, my friend."

He stood up, and there was no chair where he had been sitting.

"The air is filled with water, Jimmy. No matter where

you are, no matter where you go. The air is filled with water. You can now take that water, and turn it into ice. It sounds silly, it sounds simple, it perhaps even sounds worthless. When you embrace the Gift, however, you will never cease to be fascinated with what it can accomplish. It is called The Ice. By simply thinking it, you can form ice from the invisible water that surrounds you. You can create it in any way, shape, or form. If you can think it, it will form. Ready for your first try?"

I stared at him, trying to envision what he was talking about.

"I will now throw this rock at that wall behind you. If it hits the wall, you will suffer seven seconds of an unbearable tickling sensation."

That last phrase caught my attention.

As he had done in the past, Farmer pulled a small rock from out of nowhere. Without hesitation, he reached back and flung it at the wall behind me. Having no idea what was going on, I just watched.

When it hit the wall, I doubled over and fell to the ground. An onslaught of the worst tickling feeling I'd ever experienced swept through my body, like a million fingers of a most annoying uncle tickling me all at once. I screamed, and laughed, and writhed on the ground. Then it was gone. There was no lingering sensation.

I stood back up, gasping.

"What is this? Why would you do something like that to me?"

"I am very sorry, Jimmy. I cannot tell you how sorry I am to see you have to go through this ordeal." A smirk flashed briefly across his face, and I frowned. "But it is the only way you will learn this lesson in particular. Now, I will throw this rock again at that wall. If you do not stop it, you will suffer twenty seconds of unbearable tickling."

Somehow, the rock was again in his hands.

He threw it.

Trying to think of something, trying to make something, anything, happen, I threw all thoughts into stopping that rock. A little spurt of misty ice, about the size of an apple, formed in the palm of my hand. It was frigid, and I whipped it away, but it evaporated back into the air with a swish of cloudy air. The rock thudded against the wall.

Just as I was about to complain, the tickling started all over again. Falling to the ground, writhing once again, I flipped and flopped all over the place from the unbearable tickling. Unable to stop myself, the room was filled with the sounds of my tormented laughter. Twenty seconds seemed like twenty minutes. Finally, it stopped.

I stood up. "Farmer, this is just about the most—"

"Ah," he said, cutting me off with his outstretched hand. "Come now, Jimmy. After what we've been through thus far, don't you think it may be time to trust me?"

I nodded, still baffled at how silly the whole thing was.

"Now, we will do it again. Jimmy, The Ice is an extension of your thoughts, just like The Shield. All it takes is a thought, a notion, a whim, and you will catch this rock with your new Gift. The Ice weighs nothing. It is no burden on you. Your thoughts completely control it, holding it in place, moving it, manipulating it, bending it, relinquishing it. It is a part of you."

He paused, letting everything sink in.

"Ready?" he finally asked.

I nodded.

Again, he had the rock in his hands without any effort on his part. He reached back, and gave it a heave.

This time, my brain allowed the Second Gift to take

over. The Ice. I reached out my right hand towards the sailing rock, and *wished* it to stop.

There was a crackling, swishy sound, and a tingling in my arm. From the air around my hand, swirls of mist swarmed in from all directions, forming a tornado of white air shooting out in a line towards the rock. The mist almost instantly formed into a line of solid ice, extending from my hand all the way to the flying rock. The ice caught the rock, freezing it in its grasp, before it hit the wall.

I looked on in complete astonishment. My eyes went from the rock, frozen in a ball of solid ice, down to the shaft of ice that led to my hand, still outstretched and also covered in ice. I felt no weight. It was like the entire ice structure I had just formed ignored all laws of gravity.

With a thought, I made the ice go away. It exploded back into a swirling cloud of mist and disappeared into the surrounding air. The rock fell to the floor, two feet from the wall.

All traces of ice were gone.

I looked over at Farmer, and surprised even myself when I started to laugh.

✧CHAPTER 29✧

Short Visit

Farmer let out a slight chuckle as well, then sat back down on his invisible chair.

"Ah, Jimmy. There is still a glimmer of hope as long as we have you around. But a grave day comes, a day when battle will be joined on your world, just like it has on many others. Yet I feel we may stem the tide this time, that we may have a chance. It grieves me that no other world has had even such scant hope as you now have. It grieves me greatly."

Farmer put his fingers to his chin, taking on a look of deep thought. "Do you know why you were able to open the Door and retrieve the First Gift, establishing you as the Giftholder?" he asked.

"No," I replied, "but I guess it was because I got lucky and had the key."

Farmer shook his head adamantly. "No, it is much deeper than that. Try as they did to get the key, your enemy, the Shadow Ka, would not have been able to open the Door even if they had obtained the key. Tell me, Jimmy, why did you open the Door?"

I thought about it, then shrugged. "I didn't know what else to do."

"Did you do it to obtain the Gifts, to gain power, to save the world?"

"Well . . . no."

154

"Then why?"

Thinking back, I remembered the reason. "My whole family had been taken, and it was the only thing I could think of to do in order to save them. I didn't know what to expect beneath the Door, but I thought it was my only chance."

Farmer smiled. "You did it for one reason, and one reason only. To save your family. Think on that, and think about the intentions of the Shadow Ka. You will understand why you were successful that day."

"Farmer," I said, realizing that he didn't mind me calling him that. "Most of the things you say go right over my head. When will someone just explain to me everything that I need to know? It'd be nice to at least know what a Stomper is."

He stood up and came a step closer to me.

"Trust me on this. You must learn in small steps. Would you teach a young one just learning to walk how to perform advanced mathematics? No, you would not. It is like that."

He seemed to ponder for a moment.

"But, then again, our time is not long until the day of war comes. Each Gift will serve its own purpose at that time. Learn them well. Yes, learn them well. There are things about them that you do not yet realize. Uses that far surpass their immediate and most obvious qualities. Especially The Shield, Jimmy. I know I have told you how it can be used as a weapon, but there is something else much deeper, something tremendous.

"Also, the Stompers are not what you may now picture them to be. No, they are quite different than anything you could conjure up in that mind of yours. When you are ready to learn of them, you will be quite stunned, I assure you."

While Farmer spoke, a memory popped in my head,

something I had not thought of in a long time.

"Back in the Blackness, right after blocking the Black Curtain, what did the girl mean, when she said that she would 'die' for Joseph, after he'd been whisked away by the Shadow Ka?"

"Ah, yes, that word. I can only say that its meaning is difficult to explain, but that word is the closest we could come in your language. You see, we, the Givers, do not really exist in the sense that you understand. It is part of the greatest mystery of all, the one that you are not nearly ready enough to hear yet. Jimmy, the day comes in which you will learn something that will turn everything upside down, even more shocking than the Stompers themselves."

He leaned forward. "The greatest surprise is yet to come."

✧))✧))✧

Farmer settled back, and stared at me, seeming to enjoy the look of confusion that had to be on my face.

His head then jerked and his eyes looked into the distance, like he had just heard something.

"Our time is always so sweetly short when we meet, my friend. You must go, now, or you and your friends will be in grave danger. Practice this Gift, and you will find it to be far more powerful than you can imagine it to be, even now. Run, my boy."

His urgency took me completely off guard.

"But, wait," I said, feeling like there were too many unanswered questions lingering. "What about the other two Gifts? Where do I go? What happens next? I can't leave yet."

Farmer stepped up to me, looking very grave and certain.

"You must go to the Tower of Three Days. The remaining Gifts await you." He surveyed my face with somber eyes. "I'm sorry to add that you will be very surprised when, and if, you receive them. A guide will come to assist you and teach you more. You are ready to learn, this I can see. Now go."

A rumbling, gurgly sound came from somewhere, and the icy room began to tremble.

"What about the Stompers?" I yelled to Farmer, as the sounds got louder, a thundering of cracking ice.

"Time grows shorter," he replied. "The Stompers will be here before the next season dawns. Go. NOW!"

He pointed towards the door, which stood open, revealing the red, glowing cavern of the Pointing Finger. Confused and frightened, I made for the door. Farmer spoke once more as the cold of the room turned into the fierce heat of the volcanic cave.

"Jimmy, beware. The Stompers are not what you think. We must talk of them, soon."

I nodded, and with a pitiful wave goodbye, I reached over and slammed the wooden door closed after stepping through.

The room of ice was gone.

✧CHAPTER 30✧

The Icy Ladder

Immediately, my strange group of companions surrounded me, all yelling at the same time.

"Jimmy, the whole place is shaking! We've got to get out of here, now!"

Things were bad. No one even asked me what had just happened past the door.

The cavern was indeed shaking, enough to make us sway back and forth, stumbling into each other. Spouts of lava spewed and burst forth from cracks and fissures, like some kind of special effects show at a studio amusement park. There was no time to dilly dally, unless we wanted a nice bit of lava burn to take care of for the next few days.

As one, we sprinted for the shaft of the Finger, ignoring the fact that the slide now started a good forty feet above us. As we arrived below it, a massive jolt of quaking erupted through the entire structure, knocking us over. The sickening sound of grinding rock filled the air. The whole place seemed ready to collapse in on itself.

Rayna, her green leather reflecting the red glow of the cavern with a sickish hue, looked up towards the dangling slide and back at me, then threw her arms out for balance.

"We're finished!" she yelled. "There is no other way out. This is it!"

Thoughts thundered through my head, competing with the fear and shock of it all. The Shield was not the answer this time, even if I could have made myself sneeze. There was a new Gift, untested but hiding powers that were ready to reveal themselves. I could feel it.

"Hold on!" I yelled.

The Ice was so unlike The Shield, which required no real effort on my part. The Shield protected me, no matter what. The Ice took instruction and thought. The sensation of it still resonated throughout me—its power was there, waiting to be unleashed. It was one of the strangest things I'd ever felt.

Not sure of myself, yet realizing the predicament of the moment, I looked towards the slide. Reaching my hand upwards, I released The Ice, *pushing* it with my mind towards the sky.

Swirling tornadoes of mist drew in from all directions, forming a wavering white beam of powdery air, shooting upwards. It quickly turned into Ice, a thick, frosty rod shooting from my hand to the slide. A block of ice also formed around my hand and forearm, completely encasing them, connecting me to the beam of ice that now went from my arm to the jagged-edged bottom of the slide.

Concentrating, conjuring images of what I wanted, I forced them into the power of The Ice—the beam expanding, splitting, thickening. Everything was a rush of excitement and energy through my body. It was like drinking cold water after hours and hours in the baking sun.

Soon, without fully understanding how, above us stood a large ladder of ice. With a thought and a brief blast of mist and crackling ice, I removed my arm. The ladder hung there, solid. I had imagined it completely freezing itself to the slide way up above, and evidently it had granted my wish.

Shocked beyond words, but frantic in the circumstances, everyone began to climb with urgency. Not once did the frigid ladder quiver or crack—it was as strong as steel. Soon we arrived at the very bottom of the black slide, panting with fear and exertion. Below us, lava was pouring into the cave bottom. Cracks were forming on the sides of the shaft, sending shivers of fright through us all. Everything shook. Still, despite the heat, and despite the quaking, the Ice stayed firm.

"Okay," said Rayna, who had been first in the climb, "just do exactly as me, and you will soon find yourself at the top."

She scrambled from the ladder of ice onto the slide, and twisted around until her back was against the black stone, her head pointing up, her feet towards us, pushing against the Ice for leverage. She folded her arms across her chest, then spoke a word that sounded like Japanese.

"Ikimasho."

With a burst of speed that almost made me fall back in surprise, Rayna shot up the slide just as quickly as when we had come down. It looked for all the world like a video of our trip down, played in reverse.

Tanaka actually started giggling.

"What you think, Jimmy-san? Your little ice trick was so-so compared to that, *neh*?"

Bewildered, I watched, no less surprised, as Tanaka followed Rayna, saying the same word and shooting up the slide in reverse, defying all laws of gravity.

"Your turn." Miyoko said softly into my ear, giving me a nudge.

I climbed from the ice onto the slide, and shifted onto my back.

"What was that word again?"

"Ikimasho."

Trying my best to imitate the accent, I yelled the word,

thinking that would increase the chances of it actually working.

"Ikimasho!"

Like a slingshot, I shot upwards, sliding around and around, leaving my stomach behind at the ladder. The world spun, and nausea kicked in almost instantly. Before I could even get a good amount of screaming out, I slid up and across the top part into the arms of Rayna and Tanaka. As soon as they had me safely, Tanaka made no effort to hide his attempt to get as far away from me as possible. The two of us looked at each other and began laughing. There was nothing left for me to throw up anyway.

Seconds later, Miyoko was up, and we were ready to go.

A thunderous crack ripped through the air, and the entire Finger lurched with a jolt, knocking us from our feet. Tanaka almost fell right over the edge.

"Jimmy, do something!" Rayna yelled. "I don't think we have time to climb down, the whole thing is about to crumble to the ground!"

Panicking, I stumbled to the edge of the Pointing Finger, and peered over at the ground. The Finger was swaying back and forth, like a tree in the wind, sending waves of nausea and fright through my whole body. The whole thing must've cracked right through, way down below us. It was going to topple. Time was short.

Gripping the very edge of the Pointing Finger, I looked towards the shore, hundreds of feet away. After a deep breath, I threw every ounce of thought and energy into the power of The Ice, shouting with a fury of effort. An explosion of ice ripped through the air, streaking like a shaft of arctic lightning from me to the distant shore of the lake. The misty vapor from the air barely had time to appear before it formed the Ice, and soon, a long, wide sheet of it connected us to land.

The swaying of the Finger stopped dead. Nothing could have ever prepared me for the power of the Second Gift. The ability to form ice from air was amazing enough. But the chilling thought that it was strong enough to stop such a huge structure from falling was incomprehensible. For the first time in this whole ordeal, I felt like I was not myself, that someone had thrown the old me out the window and replaced it with a new being from the planet Krypton.

And yet, I was beginning to enjoy it.

"Come on, let's hurry, before the whole volcano explodes."

I started for the other side, ready to climb down the black spikes, when Tanaka suddenly yelled out, "Gana-barrrroooo!" and ran for the ice shaft I'd just created. Without hesitation, he jumped onto it, feet first, and began to slide down to shore. All three of us instinctively reached for him, but it was too late.

His yells of delight grew quieter as he slid further and further away. But, at last we could just see him safely reach the distant shore, and after a brief tumble, he jumped up and waved his arms like a madman.

Rayna, Miyoko, and I exchanged looks. Rayna winked at me then took off after Tanaka, sliding down the ice like a deranged, thrill-seeking kid. Then Miyoko went. When the two of them arrived safely, so far below, so far distant, there was no longer any other choice.

With a curious mix of fear and exhilaration, I crept onto the ice and pushed off. There was nothing scary about it—after the thrilling ride of a lifetime, I arrived safely onto the shore with a few tumbles and laughs.

But never in my life could I have guessed that one's bottom could get that cold.

✧CHAPTER 31✧
Jimmy Strikes Back

We quickly climbed out of the bowl wherein the lake lay, and hiked as far away as possible before collapsing with fatigue. As we sat there, the questions finally poured out concerning my trip through the door in the cavern, and I did my best to tell everyone what had happened. Needless to say, they were all quite impressed.

Since we were all so tired we agreed to rest until morning of the next day. I spent the next few hours of daylight practicing my new Gift. I could already tell it would be an invaluable asset, and I wanted to make sure it became second nature to use it. So far, The Ice had come as acts of desperation, my instinct taking over. There was still no real understanding of how it worked.

For hours on end, I used and practiced The Ice. The tingling sensation in the arms, the wispy whirls of mist and icy spray. I created blocks, beams, and balls of Ice. It took effort and concentration, tiring the mind way more than the body. Without fail, The Ice seemed to have no weight, giving me the ability to do anything I wanted. I shot great beams of Ice into the trees and held them steady, feeling light as a feather. Tanaka threw pinecones into the air and I caught them with shafts of Ice. As it came a little easier, it became more and more fun. There seemed to be no limit to what could be done with the Gift. If my mind could think it, The Ice could do it. It was in every way as amazing as The Shield.

While, playing, er, practicing, something caught my eye in the air above us.

I noticed the Sounding Rod, hovering a short distance from us. I had grown so accustomed to having it appear and disappear that it was easy to forget about. A thought swept across my mind.

Concentrating on its position, hovering there in the air, I called upon The Ice, willing it to collect and freeze around the Rod. A burst of mist and swishing air swirled around the Rod, catching it before it could escape. From end to end, it froze solid, with baby icicles coming off it in several places along its length. Then, it fell.

The Sounding Rod crashed into the ground, and with an icy clank exploded into a million pieces. Its remnants then seemed to shrivel up and evaporate into the air. Within seconds, there was nothing there, not even a trace of ice or water. It was gone.

I jumped up, suddenly excited.

"Tanaka," I screamed, "throw something at me, hit me, do something!"

He stood up and with a crooked grin came at me. Three feet in front of me, he jumped into the air, swiveling his body around until his flying foot was aimed for my head. He didn't make it far. The Shield kicked in, and Tanaka was flung back around and he fell on his head with a flump of dust.

We all cheered out loud, like we'd just won the Super Bowl.

The Sounding Rod was dead.

Once again, sneeze or no sneeze, I was invincible.

✧ ☽ ✧ ☽ ✧

The next morning, we all knew what still lay ahead for us. The search for Hood, and the rescue of my family.

Rayna pulled from her pack a rumpled, folded photograph. She flattened it out on the ground between us, and then placed her hands, palms down, on the photo's edges. She seemed to go into a deep trance, staring into the picture, almost like she was trying to see *through* it. It made me think of those computer-made 3-D pictures that took about three hours of intense staring and crossing your eyes before they would turn into some dumb image that made you wonder why in the world you had just spent all that effort and time just to see a picture of a cat with no face.

Rayna continued her scrutiny of the picture. I finally walked over and looked to see what she was looking for. It was a photograph of the leader of the Bosu Zoku, the man who had taken my family.

Kenji.

He was sitting on his bike, looking off into the distance with his eyes of coal. The photo had the date and time imprinted on the bottom right-hand corner. Then, the image *shifted*. I gasped, and leaned in for a better look.

There was suddenly a picture of Kenji on a bike, with all his followers behind him, driving down a long freeway surrounded by mountains. Even the date and time imprint had changed.

"I know where this is," Rayna said, breaking her staring contest with the picture. "This is the freeway, just over the mountain and down the ravine into the valley. We have until late afternoon three days from now to get there." She pointed to the time and the date, and I couldn't speak, dumbfounded by her ability to see the future.

"Where Kenji is, there your family will be," she said. "That gives us two full days to search for The Hooded One. If we don't find him by then, it will be too late anyway."

Rayna stood up, and stuffed the picture back into her pack.

"Didn't you say that the photo shows you several possibilities for the future?" I asked, worried about the picture I had seen in the mansion with Hood, still hoping that my future was not with certainty destined for that final end.

"You are right, Jimmy, but I probed and probed, willing it to show me the future of Kenji, and that is all that came out. My ability knows my heart, and it works to my good. It knows I wanted time to find our friend, and it knows we want to find your family. Taking all this into account, it revealed to me the most pertinent information possible. It is difficult to describe to you how it works, but it is a monumental power, one that has uses beyond anything you could conceive.

"Even though others can see the results of my power, like you did, they cannot manipulate the results like I can. When you look, you will alternate between possible future events. When I look, I see what I need to see. I see what will help me.

"That is how The Hooded One found you and waited for you in the house by the river. I knew you would be there.

"Trust me, what I have just told you is true. We have two days to find The Hooded One. Then, your family. Even if we did not need to seek out our now hoodless friend, we would be better served by waiting for three days for the Bosu Zoku to come to the place shown to me."

Remembering what my uncle Steve used to say about people who tell you how to make a clock when you ask them what time it is, I simply shrugged, and accepted her explanation.

✧Chapter 32✧
The Alliance

The next two days were ones of journey, hunger, and long stories. We scaled the mountain and countryside, looking everywhere for Hood, knowing that his chances of survival were ticking away with the clock. Raspy had mentioned him being tied to a tree, so we searched the forests from end to end, birch to pine.

Often, we split up, determining beforehand where and when to meet again. Tanaka used his skills to find us some deer and rabbit, and we ate lots of meat cooked over a humble fire. I was reminded of the old days (as old as old days can be to a fourteen-year-old) camping with the Boy Scouts. Sitting around the fire, talking and joking, had always been my favorite part of those campouts.

Now, however, the four of us didn't joke too much, as the weight of our circumstances grew heavy upon our shoulders, but we talked and talked through the night, barely sleeping. Tanaka, Miyoko, and Rayna took turns telling me the history of the Alliance, and how they all came together.

✧☽✧☽✧

The Alliance can be traced back for hundreds of years, always secret, always small. Its first member was an Ainu, a people even more ancient than the Japanese, who occupied the same land for thousands of years before people came to conquer and take it from them. They are to Japan what Native Americans are to the United States.

Slowly, the Ainu people were pushed further and further north as new settlers came to their homelands, until most of them resided in the northernmost island of Hokkaido, where we were now.

Legend has it that centuries ago, one of these Ainu was hiking in the snowy peaks of the mountains, looking for a boy of the village that was last seen wandering up the slopes. The Ainu man searched and searched, coming up vain. When in desperation he gave up, he started his way back down the icy sides of the mountain.

A sudden ripping noise, one that I had become very familiar with myself, stopped him short. Below him, a large rent in the air grew wide, engulfing the mountainside. It was blacker than the stormiest night sky, and fear overwhelmed him. In his panic, the Ainu slipped. He slid into the Blackness.

Rayna did not know for sure whether this was the first time a Random Ripping ever connected our world to the Blackness. If not the first, it surely had to be one of the earliest. The Givers were not involved yet. In fact, at the time they had not even discovered these Rippings, and their path to a world that none of them knew existed. Ours.

The Ainu man had either incredibly good luck, or incredibly bad luck, depending on how you look at it. The odds of him falling into the Blackness were astronomical, and once he was there, he had some very harrowing experiences. And yet, he survived, making it through months and months on the other side of The Black Curtain.

He encountered Shadow Ka, but luckily outran them to the iron ring-gates that led to the many worlds the

Blackness connected. He visited countless places, able to speak with many of the inhabitants, some human, some not. None of the people or creatures he encountered spoke his language, but somehow he communicated, as one does when in desperate circumstances.

Throughout his entire ordeal in the Blackness, the Ainu never once met a Giver.

But he learned and saw things that could never be forgotten.

He witnessed first hand the aftermath of the Stompers.

At that time, many worlds had still not succumbed to this path of destruction, were still fighting, however hopeless. The Ainu saw these people, before and after. Forever ingrained into his mind was the complete and unadulterated horror of this enemy.

The sunless worlds, everywhere gray. The seas of stone beds, the lifeless, yet still living inhabitants of the worlds, lying as if asleep, waiting, waiting, for who knows what, serving some purpose beyond understanding. It was complete despair to see such a thing.

But the Ainu never actually saw a Stomper, nor had anyone he communicated with. They remained a complete mystery, their secrets enshrouded within the minds of lifeless creatures who could not speak of their past. The only thing of certainty was that the gray devastation had been caused by the Stompers, their way prepared by the Shadow Ka. The hows and whys and whats, no one knew.

So, the Ainu wandered, and snuck about, and fled danger, and lived off whatever food he could find for nigh on a year. And then, in another display of his eerie luck, good or bad, he happened upon another Random Ripping, this time seeing his very own world waiting on the other side, albeit a place far from his village. He ran through, back to Earth.

It took him five years to find his way back home.

Those years would prove to be the foundation of the Alliance. As he journeyed over land and sea, mountain and plain, he gathered a following. His story was so far-fetched it was difficult to find people who would believe him. Yet he knew that there had been a purpose for his trip to the Blackness. It was up to him to prepare the world for what would eventually come. He knew the Stompers would come, would figure out a way to visit and ensnare our world, just like they had done to endless others.

He gathered the meek and the humble, the outcast and the unclean. Many had special gifts, for which they had been exiled and abandoned. He didn't know what they could do, but do something they must.

The Alliance had been born.

For centuries now, they had journeyed the earth, gathering more members for the Alliance. They sought only those who would believe, and those with gifts. Along the way, they finally met the Givers, and promised to join their efforts. There was only one requirement demanded by the Givers.

The finder of the Four Gifts must not be from the Alliance, nor helped by the Alliance until the First Gift had been discovered. It had to be so, for the person who would eventually discover and open the door in the woods, and receive the First Gift, must not be tainted with preconceived notions. Everything had been precisely planned, and specifically put into place. Everything had its purpose, and the holder of the Gifts must be one who knew nothing beforehand. He or she had to be pure in mind and heart (I blushed a little at this part), and not set in their thoughts and ways.

It had to be so, or the Giftholder would fail. The Givers were adamant. The Alliance agreed. They put their faith in such a person coming along.

It was frustrating, and ended up being almost disastrous. They had to hold back when my dad came to Japan and sought the key, for they had promised not to get involved until the Door was open. In silent frustration and fear they watched as the Shadow Ka, who were spread throughout the earth and who had done their own research of the clues left by the Givers, assisted my dad in finding the key.

At first, this seemed strange, that the Alliance would have banded against my dad. But then it hit me that back then, my dad was the bad guy, although not of his own choice. Of course the Alliance didn't want him to get the key, because then that meant the Shadow Ka would have it.

I asked Rayna the obvious question of why didn't the Shadow Ka just get it themselves if they knew so much. She explained that there were two answers to my question. One, the Ka did not simply know everything. They were figuring it out just like anyone else, trying to find the key and the Door and the Gifts before a human did. But, they also knew that in the end, only a human could get the key, and open the Door, and receive the Gifts. They either wanted to stop it all together, or find a human they could convince to receive it and work for them, not against them.

Well, in the end, it had worked out for the good. It looked like the Givers knew what they were talking about after all.

I had opened the Door, and now had the first two Gifts. I told them about my conversation with Farmer back at the Pointing Finger, when he said I was able to open the Door in the woods because of my intent. Rayna rhetorically asked us what could be more pure than wanting to save your family. A long silence followed, and my heart was full.

✧⟩✧⟩✧

So now I knew the history of the Alliance. Rayna, Miyoko, Hood, Tanaka, and Geezer all joined eventually, led there by different paths and through different circumstances. Miyoko's was the easiest, since her dad, Tanaka, was a member. There were others throughout the world, fulfilling their various duties, preparing the way for me to succeed in obtaining the Gifts, and preparing the world for the battle that was sure to come.

After the talk, there was something that I no longer had any doubt about.

Just as the fate of the world would eventually rest on my shoulders, so would it on those of this group.

The Alliance.

✧Chapter 33✧

Very Unexpected Events

In our spare time of resting and eating, I was learning new tricks with my two Gifts. Never having forgotten Farmer's words that someday I would realize how The Shield could also be used as a weapon, I began to think about a couple of experiences I'd had when The Shield had protected me. Back when I went to my house after having been through The Door, and found my family there, Raspy's goon, Monster, tried to shoot me. The bullet ricocheted violently, exploding my mom's sweet little reading lamp. If that direction of rebounding could be controlled . . .

Over and over during our meal breaks, I threw rocks up into the air and tried to manipulate how The Shield rebounded them away from me. Slowly, but surely, I got the hang of it. And with a burst of intense thinking, I was able to make The Shield rebound objects harder and harder. Soon, I was able to throw a rock into the air, and when it fell towards me and hit The Shield, I *threw* it back, concentrating on where I wanted it to go.

Again, Tanaka was my assistant. We set up a stack of logs, and then Tanaka would throw boulders or other discarded objects right at me. Sort of like a soccer goalie heading a shot out of bounds, I would deflect the objects with a burst of thought, and they would explode with speed towards the stack of logs, knocking them over. Before too long, I had become an expert, and never missed. Within a matter of two days, I felt like I had picked up two valuable weapons to use in our battle against the Shadow Ka, and ultimately the Stompers, although there was still the mystery of the other uses of the Gifts that Farmer had not elaborated on.

The Ice. The Shield. It was almost becoming fun. But then thoughts of our predicament brought me crashing back to reality. The Gifts were not for my amusement. Their sole purpose was to assist me in an undertaking that was probably unprecedented in our little history of Earth. From what I could tell, terrible things were in store for all of us.

In the evening of the second day of our search, as I tried my best to battle such gloomy thoughts so that I could actually get some sleep, I again committed to myself that I would do everything possible to be ready for what lay ahead. Eventually, although I have no memory of when, I fell asleep.

✧)✧)✧

On the morning of the third day, the skies were filled with dark and heavy clouds, gray and sinister. Thunder rumbled above, and the light of the sun seemed to have fled as far away as possible. In these conditions, we came upon a forest that seemed darker than night within its tightly packed trees, thick and looking untouched by human hands for ages.

"This will be our last chance," said Rayna as we divided ourselves into search groups. Her distorted face and one eye looked more weary than usual. "We must leave here within three hours if we are to get the horses and make it to the place where we will meet the Bosu Zoku."

"Maybe we shouldn't split," I suggested. "We can't take

a chance of missing the opportunity to find my family."

"I agree," said Miyoko. "The Hooded One may not have survived this long anyway, as hard as that may be to accept. Let's not lose Jimmy's family as well."

Tanaka agreed with his daughter, and Rayna reluctantly accepted. So, as one, we entered the gloomy sea of trees.

The leaves, moss, and twigs of the forest floor were damp and spongy, making almost no sound as we trampled forward. The tall, heavily branched trees seemed to suck in sound, so that a thick silence filled the air. We moved deeper into the woods, looking in all directions for any sign of Hood.

Then, I had just about the craziest ten minutes of my life.

✦ ☽ ✦ ☽ ✦

Rayna suddenly screamed at the top of her lungs, the wailing sound seeming to echo in the still air, dulled but loud.

In the seconds before we realized the source of her fear, my mind raced, because the sound of her scream was so familiar. It was not the first time I had heard that scream, I was sure of it.

And then it clicked, and I understood the second amazing fact about Rayna.

Often, sounds or smells bring back memories, vividly, so that it's almost like you're there again. The sound of that scream did it to me. I felt like I was in another set of woods, far away, all over again. I could almost smell the familiar scent of the wood and leaves of a certain tree in Georgia, and feel the faint breeze as I swayed with the tree in its uppermost branches. The image of Mayor Duck, dragging a woman through the woods, fighting against her struggles, popped in my head. I again felt the fear of that first day, the day this whole mess started. I remembered her scream.

Rayna.

Rayna was the woman. I was sure she had died, that the mayor had killed her and then dropped her into the Blackness.

Rayna was the woman.

Snapping back to reality, I frantically looked around. I didn't know which was stranger—that Rayna had pulled a Joseph and come back from the dead, or that she just happened to be standing in front of me again, in the middle of a Japanese forest, screaming.

It all barely registered, flashing through my mind in an instant.

Then I noticed the source of Rayna's fright, a fifteen-foot tall monkey.

I decided to scream too.

✧ ☽ ✧ ☽ ✧

It was not a gorilla. It was a monkey. A gangly, hairy, unusually large monkey.

It sat hunched over, its back against a tree with precious few branches, more closely resembling a telephone pole than a tree. The monkey looked tired and beat. Its massive head shifted, and the monkey looked at us. Suddenly realizing that a battle with a gargantuan primate was the absolute last thing I wanted that day, I made to run back in the direction we had come from. But Tanaka grabbed my hand, and put his finger to his lips, shushing me.

Rayna also calmed down, and took a step backwards, huddling closer with the rest of us. We continued to stare at the tall beast. Amazingly, my shock at realizing the identity of Rayna had already worn off, replaced by the shock of seeing a monkey five times the size it was supposed to be. The monkey was ancient, with most of its hair gray, and everything about it looking old and withered.

Tanaka took a step forward, and then slowly turned around to face us. He spoke in a quiet whisper, shot with barely contained excitement.

"You realize what this is? We are first people in history to witness this!"

"What?" I asked back.

"This is an *okisaru*!"

I looked over at Miyoko.

She shrugged, then said, "It means *Big Monkey*."

Shocking even myself, I laughed out loud.

"That's ingenious, Tanaka."

"You don't understand," he said back, not appreciating my sarcasm. "These creatures are of an ancient myth that only a few people even know about! Not one person on the earth could have possibly believed that one actually exists. They are supposed to hold great powers, beyond the greatest thinker's imagination."

Tanaka looked back at the *okisaru*, and knelt on one knee.

The giant monkey leaned forward, and his tired eyes looked deep into Tanaka's. The creature then raised his right arm, and held out one finger, pointing it at Tanaka. It brought the finger forward until it was touching Tanaka's forehead. They both closed their eyes, and the rest of us could only stare, left to wonder what in the heck was happening.

Seconds stretched into minutes.

The monkey drew his hand away. Tanaka opened his eyes, and fell backwards, into Rayna's arms. There was an indescribable look of wonder on his face.

Then, in an instant, the monkey flung himself up into the trees and was gone, moving with a speed that seemed impossible. After a few seconds of rustling branches and swaying tree trunks, it was as if the beast had never been there.

Tanaka stood up and walked forward, continuing his search for Hood. For the rest of that day, he would say nothing of his experience.

As the rest of us followed, I tried to think if I'd ever had a stranger ten minutes than what I'd just experienced. First, realizing who Rayna was, then, an enormous monkey of some ancient legend touching my new friend in the forehead with its finger, then disappearing into the trees.

Not until many weeks later would I realize the unbelievable magnitude of what had just happened.

✧CHAPTER 34✧

The Unhooded One

Putting it in the backs of our minds as best we could, we continued the search for Hood, creeping slowly through the dim, soundless forest. As we trudged along, weary from pushing through heavy growth and being hit in the face by prickly branches, I wanted to ask Rayna about that day in Georgia, even though I realized it might be a touchy subject. I also wondered if that terrible day explained some of her face's disfiguration, and if the memory of it would be too difficult for her. But my desire to make sure she knew that I had figured it out overcame my hesitation.

"Rayna, that was you in Georgia that day?"

Perhaps still shaken by our sight of the mysterious monkey as well, her tone suggested that she was not in much of a mood to talk about it. "I figured you would realize who I was eventually," she said. "Surely you didn't think that was just some random woman snooping around for The Door, did you?"

"Well, I didn't know a thing about any of this back then, and I sure didn't know you or about the Alliance, so how on earth was I supposed to guess that the woman I saw must be a weird lady with special powers from an Alliance of strange people with gifts, tramping about the world trying to figure out how they can help a group called The Givers, who are from another world, save us all from a ruthless enemy?"

Rayna gave me her already familiar look of motherly disapproval.

"Weird?" she asked.

"What?"

"Weird. You called me weird. I don't appreciate that."

Rolling my eyes, I said, "Anyway, Rayna, what were you doing there?"

"The Alliance sent me. We wanted to learn more about The Door, and the Givers find it difficult to tell us anything. So I went. We knew that your father had taken the key to America, and that it was hidden, but we were worried that somehow it would still end up in the hands of the Shadow Ka. We wanted to do something, although we had no idea what. So, I went. That blubbering fool, Duck, found me, and dragged me to a Random Ripping to drop me into The Blackness. I can't believe he was dumb enough to think I was dead—I was faking it."

"Well, from what I've learned, you maybe could've been dead and still been okay."

"What're you talking about?"

"My friend, Joseph. He was healed by The Blackness, and so was my dad. It heals."

"Yes, yes, we've heard that myth. Are you telling me that it's true?"

"Absolutely," I said, surprised that she didn't know that. "So what happened after you went into The Blackness? Was that your first time there?"

"It was not my first. The tale of my first trip there will have to be saved for another time."

Rayna took on a heavy look of grief, and her eyes were filled with a memory of horror or pain. I didn't push the issue.

"How did you make it back here to Japan?"

"The girl. The little girl Giver. She brought me to a Ripping, and pushed me through. She was the one who told me about you, although it would've been impossible for her to know yet what you would end up becoming."

"Well," I replied, "you can see the future with your photographs, so why would it be so strange for her to be able to do the same, some other way?"

"You're right. There are so many things about The Givers that we have yet to learn."

Our conversation dwindled into contemplative silence after that, and we continued our walking and searching.

One hour later, literally minutes before our self-imposed deadline to give up, we found The Hooded One.

✧))✧))✧

Our first sight of him was a glimmer of white in the distance, like some haunted vision of a ghost in the woods. Soon, it was obvious to the others that it was Hood in the distance, tied to a tree. Miyoko turned to me, and put her hand on my chest.

"Jimmy, stay here. Let us go and tend to The Hooded One, and put his robe back on him. You do not want to see him without it."

"Why?"

"There is something about him that we have not told you."

Without explaining, she joined the others and went off into the distance. Not wanting to challenge her advice, I sat down on the damp forest floor and rested.

A few minutes later, Miyoko, Tanaka, and Rayna walked back to me. Tanaka pulled me up from my sitting position. Standing behind them, his face hidden in the shadows of his dirty brown robe, was Hood. The red Bender Ring was at his side, supporting some of his weight.

With a slight bow of his head, Hood stepped close to a tree, and extended his pale white hand and finger to write a message.

"THANK YOU, JIMMY, FOR COMING FOR ME."

His painted words were sloppy on the bark of the tree, but the message tore into my heart. This strange person, hiding from the world behind cloth and grime, capable of powers that defied human understanding, had truly become my friend.

"There was never another option," I said, embarrassed at the slight quiver in my voice.

And with that being enough, the five of us made our way to the other side of the mountain to find our horses.

Along the way, I asked Rayna to tell us the story of her other trip to the Blackness before the one in which Duck sent her there. Unfortunately, she obliged.

✧CHAPTER 35✧

The Eye of Goo

After Rayna's parents died and left her stranded, a homeless girl in a foreign country, she had learned many tough lessons while living in the streets. A rough life had left her in the condition that I knew her—ugly, scarred, and cheerless. Her life quickly reached a point in which living it out to the end seemed a miserable option.

Then, in her late teens, a miracle occurred that saved her life and gave meaning to it all at once. While digging through the trash on a humid summer day, she came across a stack of photographs. With nothing but time on her hands, Rayna took the photos and sat down in the alley, taking the time to look through them and dream of a better life, one that was worth capturing for the ages on film.

She soon noticed that the pictures must have been thrown out as a mistake—they were all of a birthday party for the little boy who lived in the apartments near the alley where she usually slept. They were all such happy moments, full of laughter, wrapping paper, and cake. She examined each one, and it lifted her spirits. She felt, almost, like the people were her own family. One by one, she lightly brushed her fingers across the photos, the closest she would ever get to feeling the warm touch of loved ones.

When she was done, she packed them away, deciding that the family needed those pictures much less than she did. From that time on, she intended to hold on to them with every ounce of life she had—they would become her family of sorts, her way of escaping and pretending there were people who cared for her.

Later that day, after the usual turmoil of life on the street, Rayna excitedly found a secluded spot and called on her new family once again. She made herself comfortable, whipped the photos out of her tattered bag, and began her visit.

What she saw then, in those abandoned photographs, set her life on a new course.

The boy, falling off his bike, a look of terror on his face.

The boy, graduating from high school.

The boy, eating in a restaurant, driving a car, watching TV.

His parents, his friends, his siblings, all doing an assortment of things, none of them important, but changing her life nonetheless. The pictures kept changing, some even as she looked directly at them. Some even ended up showing means of death. They altered enough as she flipped through them that she knew right away that not everything she saw could possibly come true.

Rayna was homeless, Rayna was ugly, Rayna was unhappy, but Rayna was not stupid. She knew that the world was different now, that she had discovered a special gift that changed everything. She did not need to find the Alliance, they found her, and she joined without hesitation.

Tanaka, Geezer, many others. There was one precious meeting with the Givers. Her life found meaning. She now had purpose. With no hesitation, Rayna devoted her life to the future of the world, and engaged herself in the battle against the Stompers.

Every member of the Alliance had one goal to make

their calling official—a visit to the Blackness. Rayna's came fourteen years after her initial experience with the photographs.

The Givers had given them a time and a place, and Rayna waited anxiously for the Random Ripping. It was a quiet spot near a river, a journey of some days from where she was living. Eventually, the sound of ripping paper and static electricity filled the air around her, and she jumped through. Rayna was in the Blackness.

The black marble path stretched out before her, surrounded by the mercurial waters, gently ebbing against the slightly raised path. Mist and cloud filled the air and sky, silent and wet. She began to walk.

On and on she went, passing the round, stone landings holding the stack of iron rings that served as gateways to other worlds. Rayna passed by them, not yet knowing at the time what their purpose was. Later, she would wonder why the Givers had not given her more instruction before sending her in. It would prove to be a reason that she did not want. Rayna was there to have a specific experience, one that would help the cause of the Alliance, one that would give them invaluable knowledge.

An experience that would haunt her dreams from that time forward.

She had been walking for hours, tired and hungry, wishing miserably to go home. The Blackness was not turning out the way she expected. There was no glamour, nothing bizarre or fascinating. It was just black marble, a sea of inky water, and fog.

The piercing sound of the Shadow Ka hit her ears before the sight of it hit her eyes. Dread dropped over her, and she quickly hunkered down to the path, crouching, hoping against hope that it would not see her. Knowing it would be impossible not to look, her eyes flickered through the sky, timorous and weak. She was petrified.

A slight disturbance in the fog, shooting eddies of mist in all directions, announced the arrival of the Ka. Its massive, black shadowed wings thumped the moist air, and when it spotted Rayna, the Shadow Ka let out another painful cry.

Rayna did the only thing that human instinct teaches someone when a big bad shadow monster is coming at you. She got up and ran.

The Ka swooped down and grabbed her with its dark claws, grasping the back of her shirt, not letting go. With a yelp, Rayna felt herself lifted into the air, the ground quickly being swallowed up in the thick fog. Her stomach lurched from the speed and height and terror.

The Shadow Ka flew and flew, until finally, it reached its home.

Then, it got scary.

✧☽✧☽✧

As they flew, Rayna settled a bit, realizing that for the moment the Ka was not going to hurt her, and its grip on her was not painful, although uncomfortable. Feeling very absurd, she just hung there, looking in the direction of their flight, anxious about what awaited them.

In the distance, a great darkness loomed. Soon, it took on definition—massive, humongous, and unbelievable to her eyes.

Her mind could not interpret what she was seeing. It kept computing that what she saw was impossible. But there it was. It was so large, it filled her whole vision as they flew closer, a black, writhing mass of shiny, gooey something. Although she had no idea what it was made of, the form and shape of the structure was absolutely unmistakable. It was a face, its identity certain.

As they approached it, it became more and more difficult to see all of the features on the face. The eyes were suddenly miles above her, the mouth miles below, and the nose directly in front, coming closer and closer. Its surface moved and shook, like tar in an earthquake.

With a scream, the Shadow Ka suddenly swooped upwards. Now they were flying towards the eyes of the massive black carving. Then, towards one eye. Before long, it was obvious that the Ka was not going to slow down, that it meant to fly into the eye. Soon the orb was upon them.

Rayna screamed as they plunged into the black goo of the eye.

The eye of the face that looked very familiar.

It was hers.

✧ ☽ ✧ ☽ ✧

Rayna felt the Shadow Ka let go. Suddenly, she was floating in emptiness, nothingness. All around her, images shifted in and out, appearing here, appearing there, some flickering for a second, then gone, some staying for several seconds. They were all images of her life, of her dreams, of her nightmares. They were memories of both the real world and her sleeping world. They were all bad, all terrifying. Everything in her mind that was worth forgetting, that needed forgetting, flew past her, reminding her, haunting her.

She felt so exhausted. She wanted to sleep. She wanted to give up, give in to this madness and be done with it.

Then, there was a face in front of her, yelling at her.

The person slapped Rayna, jolting her awake.

It was a lady, a beautiful lady, all dressed in shiny green.

She was yelling something.

"I will die for you! Use this chance that I have given you!"

She then put her hands over Rayna's eyes, and the world exploded around her, with no sound, but violent all the same.

She opened her eyes, and she was standing once again on the marble path, in the middle of the silvery sea. Soon after, a Ripping opened, and she stepped through. The dreary world of the Blackness was replaced with the familiar streets of Japan.

The nightmare was over, Rayna was home.

All I could think about was Joseph. He was still in that horrible place.

✧ ☽ ✧ ☽ ✧

Talk about your downer stories. I decided right then that I was going to take a break from asking people about their pasts. If people wanted me to know something, they could offer it up without telling me the whole depressing story. Yikes.

"From that day on," Rayna concluded, "I have always worn green, in honor of that lady who saved me. I don't know what she meant by saying she would die for me, but whatever she did, it helped me escape a terror that I could never describe to you adequately. Please, let's forget it, and not speak of it again. There is much to do."

More than happy to grant her request, we all took a deep breath and continued on toward the horses.

✦ ⟩ ✦ ⟩ ✦

They were right where we left them, although nearly out of food. There didn't seem to be a blade of grass or a single leaf in sight. They had taken pretty good care of themselves. Running behind schedule, we got them ready in a hurry, and took off down the mountain. Luckily for us, our destination lay in the opposite direction of the way we had come. Otherwise, we would've had a dandy of a time getting around the disaster of the mudslide.

We picked our way down trails, through crevices and gullies, traipsing our way through bush and jagged stone. Eventually, finally, we burst out of a ravine upon a wide valley that stretched for miles until it hit another mountain range in the distance. There, in the middle of the valley before us, wound a long ribbon of black. The freeway that Rayna had spoken of. We had made it to the place in the picture—even I could see that.

To our right, way in the distance, we could see a pack of something slowly moving down the freeway towards the road directly below us.

"There they are." Rayna said simply, no need to clarify.

"Jimmy," Miyoko said in a somber voice. I turned my attention towards her.

"You are now a member of the Alliance. No, you are now the leader of the Alliance. We will join with you and we will defeat the Stompers. We will go where you lead, we will do what you say, we will fight who you fight. With you, we will gather the others of our alliance, we will help you obtain the Third and Fourth Gifts, and we will save the world."

I stared at her, at all of them. I now knew that I was indeed a pretty important person, but this seemed a bit much. I was embarrassed.

"Okay, Miyoko. Thanks, I guess. We're all in this together, and somehow we'll make it through. But right now, all I can think of is my family, and according to Rayna, they're down there, with those scary people on motorcycles. It's time to go get them."

"Well, what is our plan of action?" asked Rayna. "If we come at them from different—"

"No," I cut her off, looking down at the approaching army of Shadow Ka. "I can't afford to spend half my time trying to protect you guys with my Gifts. Stay here and rest."

I looked back at them, and surprised myself with my next words.

"I'll be much more powerful if I'm alone."

With that, I turned my horse towards the valley below, looking once again at the gathered mass of motorcycles. I gave Baka a gentle kick.

✧CHAPTER 36✧

The Joust of Ice and Shadow

I headed straight for the freeway, about a mile ahead of where the Bosu Zoku were packed together, slowly moving down the road towards me, weaving in and out of each other, revving their engines, loud even from the distance. Miyoko had told me about these guys, and how they often disrupted traffic, acting like they ruled the world. I could see cars behind them turning around, and others simply pulling off to the side and getting out to watch whatever was planned. It all seemed so strange.

I rode hard down the long path, wondering when they would see me and what they would do then. Finally, I reached the wide road, slowed Baka down, and trotted to the middle of the paved freeway, turning towards the Bosu Zoku.

I stared at them, my heart racing, trying to sort out what in the world I thought I was going to do, reminding myself that they had my family somewhere, and that this was the only way to save them.

Ever so slowly, the riders came closer. As they approached, I could see that we had far underestimated their numbers. There had to be at least fifty of them. Fifty motorcycles, with Shadow Ka as their riders.

Two things kept me strong. The sure knowledge that the Sounding Rod was destroyed, and the incredible new gift I had received. No matter what these people attempted, they

would not hurt me. I had a newfound courage that far sur-
passed anything I'd felt before. I was ready for them.

A sudden surge in the sounds of their engines ripped
through the air.

They had seen me, and they knew who I was.

A new focus came over the group, the random weav-
ings and the errant shouts coming to a halt. As one, they
lined up in rows covering the entire four-lane road. There
appeared to be a larger shape in the middle of the pack, but
it was too far away to tell for sure. With a roar they brought
their bikes up to full speed, and charged.

Adrenaline filled me.

With a yell I kicked Baka into action. He let loose, galloping with all of his strength, bursting forward in his own
charge, heading straight for the Bosu Zoku.

It seemed impossible to go so fast on a horse. Wind
ripped at my hair and clothes. An assortment of sounds
filled my ears, almost deafening. The clacking of the hooves
on the road, the roar of the wind, the piercing scream of
the bike engines.

We charged on, as did they, the gap between us narrow-
ing by the second. Their motorcycles tore down the road,
coming and coming, their awful sounds getting louder and
louder. I urged Baka on, trying to breathe, to stay calm.

From above it must have been quite a sight. A massive
body of motorcycles charging towards a lone horse and
rider, galloping with matched determination, both groups
on a certain collision course.

One biker broke off from the group, revving his engine
with a quick wheelie and then bursting ahead of the others.
The speed was incredible. They were now only a couple of
football fields away.

Then, I had an idea, and went with it.

✧ ❱✧❱✧

My family once went to a place where you sat in a huge arena, and watched men dressed like medieval knights pretend to fight while you ate dinner. It was a blast, and my favorite part had been the jousting tournament, where armored knights charged each other on horses, trying to knock the other off with a long, thick, spear-like thing called a lance.

Right then, approaching the biker, it was all I could think of.

I called upon The Ice. It was still an effort, difficult on a galloping horse, and I was glad for those hours of practice. I felt invincible.

I put forth my right hand, pointing toward the lone biker. That soft crackling sound fluttered through the air, followed by the tingling sensation of The Ice. It enveloped my entire arm, still pointed straight ahead, and I then *pushed* it forward. Molecules of water swarmed out of the air in a misty cloud, quickly forming a long javelin of ice extending out from my arm, five inches thick, seven feet long, and tapering down to a pointed end. I charged forth like an ancient knight of England, right arm extended, the cold shaft of my frozen lance ready for combat.

As strange as the whole thing seemed, it got stranger.

The biker was now in plain sight, maybe fifty yards away. His bandanna flapped in the wind, as did his hair. Sunglasses hid eyes that I knew to be pitch black. A wicked grin filled his face. And then he revealed himself to be a monster.

He held out his right hand, and it exploded into a swirling tornado of black ash, spinning and spinning until it was a formless beam of dark shadow. It extended toward me, until he too appeared to be holding a lance. His was black, mine was the color of wet crystal.

With no time to ponder the surreal craziness of it all, I charged full speed ahead.

Twenty yards.

The scream of his engine drowned out the pounding of Baka's hooves.

Fifteen yards.

I leaned forward, tightening every muscle in my right arm. He did the same, the grin never leaving his face.

Ten yards.

With a gasp of surprise, coming too late, I realized his lance was longer than mine.

It crashed into The Shield, dissolving into swimming specks of shadow. It didn't rebound like most objects do. It just disintegrated two feet in front of me, his dark lance disappearing bit by bit as it hit The Shield.

My lance of ice reached him. The tip of it tore into his leather-jacketed shoulder, ripping him off the bike and throwing him into the air. He let out a scream that belied his macho image and landed with a horrible thump, his bike skittering to a halt behind us.

I released The Ice, and it exploded with a swirl of mist back into the air.

I jumped off of Baka, and gave him a quick push, urging him to get away as fast as possible. His job done, he galloped away, off towards the mountain above us.

I turned around and faced the rest of the oncoming mob.

It was time for battle.

✧CHAPTER 37✧

A Sea of Bikes

I needed to stop them if I was going to figure out where my family was being held. Having seen what I did to their lead man, surely they realized there was nothing they could do to hurt me. Rayna had foreseen a sense of urgency in the photo, that they were on their way somewhere important, so after what I did to the first biker, they probably formed a new strategy of just going right by and leaving me behind. I couldn't let that happen.

Of course, these thoughts went through my head in an instant.

The first row of Bosu Zoku was twenty yards away. Their deadly stares bore down on me, and I could feel their hatred. I called upon The Ice.

I brought both arms up from my sides, holding them straight out, pointing away from me in both directions, as if I were ready to give a welcoming hug to my friends on the bikes.

The crackling sound of ice forming filled the air, misty swirls of moisture shooting out from my hands. The Ice covered my arms completely, and I was able to push it with less effort than ever before, blasting from my hands in a straight line, forty inches thick, forming a barrier chest-high across the entire freeway. Without any specific thought from me, The Ice obeyed my wishes and floated there, again defying gravity. Once the ends of the thick rods of ice reached the edges of the freeway, I planned to expand them into a solid wall. But they had just reached those points when my eyes caught something that made my stomach turn over.

As I stood there, the first bikers just feet away from the deadly line of ice, I realized that among them was a red car, a sporty sedan, with a certain passenger in the back seat.

Mom.

It all happened so fast, the Bosu Zoku didn't have time to swerve or hit their brakes. They set themselves on breaking through or dying in the attempt.

In horror, in that split instant, I realized that crashing into the ice at that speed would be certain disaster for my mom in the car.

Inches away now, some of the surrounding bikers were chickening out and dropping to the ground in an attempt to play limbo with the ice. I caught a quick glimpse of my mother's face staring ahead, her eyes filled with terror.

Before the thought even took true form in my head, I exploded The Ice into oblivion, just in time. The misty explosion covered the windshield of the sedan like it had been bombed with a water balloon.

I caught another bike from the corner of my eye, noticing Rusty seated on the back. I could see his arms around the biker, tied with rope, gripping the leather jacket of the Bosu Zoku. There was no way he could jump off, not that he would if he could at that speed.

It all seemed a blur. In that same second of time, I also saw my dad on the back of another bike zooming along on the other side of Mom's car. Soon, the very people I had come to save would be long gone, with no way to follow.

An instinct I didn't realize was there took over.

I shot a beam of ice straight towards the back of Mom's car as she passed, freezing it solid to the bumper on the back. I didn't want them to wreck, so I let The Ice expand in a line as the car moved forward. I quickly formed a large plate of Ice below me, like a wide, thick skateboard. I froze it around my feet, making sure plenty of ice was between them and the ground. Then I stopped the expansion of the line of Ice, and my whole body shot forward like a rocket as I trailed the vehicle. The beam of ice held me solidly attached to the bumper, the plate of ice skimming the ground below me. I kept forming ice on the bottom of the plate as it eroded against the pavement.

With the sudden addition of all the weight, the car slowed a bit before climbing back up to speed.

With seconds now to actually think, I couldn't believe what I was doing. I was skiing behind a speeding car with a rope and board made of ice.

The driver tried swerving to break the long line of ice. I was way ahead of him. The Ice had become part of me, obeying me before I could form thoughts. The Ice liquefied and reformed with every move, becoming a fluid rope as we made our way down the freeway.

Then, the other bikers got involved.

From every direction, Bosu Zoku converged on me and the rope of ice, intent on breaking it.

A big guy came in from the left. With my free hand I shot a blast of ice at his wheels, instantly freezing them. He tumbled and rolled. Skinny guy from the right. Another blast of ice. He flipped into the air, screaming as we flew past.

Two more from the left, three from the right. I pushed thick streams of ice in both directions, hitting all of them at the same time. They tumbled and smashed into each other, skidding straight for me. I blasted a line of ice to the ground like a rocket, shooting myself up into the air to let them pass under me. At the same time, the rope of ice in front of me continued its fluid forming and reforming. I came back down as I released the rocket pillar of ice back into the air. My skateboard of ice thickened, supporting me as I continued down the road, trailing the car.

Rusty looked back at me. I didn't have time to yell or smile.

More and more bikes were coming. With every ounce of effort in my body, I tracked them all and shot out streams of ice to knock them over. Still more came, from every direction. Some were foolish enough to attack, only to find themselves flung away like trash when they hit The Shield.

Ice was shooting from me nonstop, blasting this way and that, almost out of control. One after the other, I kept them away from my rope of ice. Five to the left. Six to the right. Bikes and bodies tumbled and bounced all around me. Screams and taunts and roaring engines and screeching brakes and skidding tires and scraping metal filled the air. I was in chaos.

Still more came. They were like army ants.

Terrified, I realized these people were not afraid to die. The Shadow Ka were in control, and they swarmed in a kamikaze attempt to overwhelm me. Ten or more came in from each side, all at once, all aimed straight for the rope of ice in an attempt to destroy it. With a scream I blasted ice in every direction.

It was not enough.

As bodies and bikes flew in every direction, one got through.

He flew through the rope, shattering it with such force that I couldn't reform it in time.

My line broken, I flew forward head first, the plate of ice attached to my feet releasing into the air with a misty explosion.

I bounced along the ground like I was in a bubble, The Shield protecting me completely.

I got up and stared ahead. My heart dropped in despair watching the car and the few bikes that had made it through the onslaught storm ahead in a mad rush, leaving me behind.

I had been so close.

✧CHAPTER 38✧

Fast

My family gone, I looked around me. People were squirming and groaning on the ground in every direction. The bikes lay scattered everywhere, solid ice attached to all of them in different places. Then I realized I had over-looked the obvious answer to my dilemma.

The bikes.

I ran to the closest one, released the ice from it, and pulled it up onto its wheels. A Bosu Zoku near the bike said something mean in Japanese, but I ignored him.

I'd ridden dirt bikes with my cousins plenty of times, but these things were completely different. I had no choice. I had to try.

I pushed a button and it started right up. I swung my leg over the seat, and took a deep breath. Then, I straight-ened my back, stared ahead, and twisted the throttle.

The bike shot out from under me with a loud scream, screeching and skidding forward as I fell straight down onto my bottom. The Shield didn't protect me as much as usual, as if to say I deserved it.

I got up and ran to the bike, ready to try again.

This time, I leaned forward, and pulled back on the gas very slowly. It moved forward, and I increased the speed as I gained more confidence. Knowing that The Shield would protect me if I were to wreck, I quickly got the hang of it, going faster and faster until it felt like I'd been shot from a cannon. The wind ripped at my body, the roar of it deafening. The ear-splitting scream of the bike was like nails on a chalkboard.

I took it to its fastest speed. One big bump, one small mistake, and I would fly through the air like Superman. I wouldn't be hurt, but the bike might not survive, and then I would truly be done with my chase. With every bit of effort I could call forth, I concentrated on controlling the bike and gaining ground on the Bosu Zoku and my family.

Thinking I was down and out, they must have slowed, because I soon spotted them in the distance. They were like glimmering buildings on the horizon, with the distant mountains rising up beyond them. Hoping they didn't notice me, I rode on.

The road flew past below me, the trees a blur on both sides. It soon felt like I was in a different world, growing numb to the sensation of speed.

Gaining on them, I could now make out their shapes. I could just see the two members of my family clinging to their captors, and the car with my mom in it.

My eyes began to water, and I wiped them with my shoulders, not daring to let go with one of my hands. I had only been blinded for a moment, but when I looked again they were gone.

No. They had just driven off the freeway, to the right. I caught sight of them again. They had come to a stop and were getting off the bikes and out of the car. For some reason, there appeared to be a big dust storm surrounding them. Dread filled me.

There was a big shape behind them, hard to make out. I kept up my speed, racing ahead, desperate to get there.

As I topped a slight rise in the road, it became clear what the object was. I couldn't believe it. The resources

of this band of thugs were becoming more and more baf-
fling.

There, in the clearing, its blades beating the air around
it, stirring dust in all directions, was something my new
bike would never catch.

A helicopter.

✧☽✧☽✧

Now truly desperate, I gunned the bike with a last burst
of effort. I could see them getting on the helicopter, forcing
my family members to do the same. The bad guys looked
in my direction, surely with sneers even though I couldn't
see them well enough.

I reached the point where they had driven off of the
road, having to slow down considerably to turn and drive
towards them. They were so close. I revved the bike and
shot towards them, but I knew I wouldn't make it.

The last person jumped on, and the helicopter slowly
lifted from the ground.

I skidded to a halt and leaped from the bike, running the
last few steps to where the huge flying vehicle had just been
resting. I stared up at it, squinting to keep the dust from
my eyes, wanting to scream and cry at the same time.

Dad's head poked out of the side door and looked down
at me, sadness filling his eyes, before he was jerked back
inside.

Then another face looked down at me as the helicopter
reached a point forty feet above me. Even from that distance, I could tell there were no whites in the eyes of that
face. And I recognized that horrible grin.

Kenji.

I decided to try my new trick with The Shield. I formed
a ball of ice, and threw it up in the air. As it fell toward my

head, I concentrated on The Shield, weaving thoughts into it, thinking I wanted the ice to rebound and shoot towards the chopper. A foot above me, it bounced off of The Shield and shot towards the helicopter with breathtaking speed. It whipped past it, barely missing.

Kenji laughed, waved, and then yelled down to me, his words barely perceptible.

"Jimmy-san! You can either continue your pointless search for the Gifts, or you can try to find where I am taking your family! Your choice!"

With that, he ducked back into the helicopter with a final, demeaning wave.

I realized shooting at the chopper was a stupid idea anyway. I couldn't take a chance of hurting my family.

It was then that I had one of the craziest ideas of my life, even by the new Jimmy Fincher's standards.

✧CHAPTER 39✧

To See From Above

The helicopter had risen to about fifty yards, and was starting to turn itself around, ready to fly away. They would be gone in seconds.

Staring through the swirling dust at the rising helicopter, I made my arms go rigid, slightly apart from the sides of my body, pointing down. I called upon The Ice, immediately feeling the tingling and hearing the crackling. As it formed around my hands, I asked myself if I really wanted to do this, then decided there was nothing to lose.

I had always wanted to fly.

✧)✧)✧

Taking a deep breath, checking one last time to see exactly where the chopper was, I exerted every bit of my mental strength into throwing a command at The Ice. This would far surpass anything I'd done so far with the second Gift.

From both arms, I pushed The Ice in a massive, explosive blast towards the ground below me. Two thick, icy pillars thundered into the ground, and my body shot skywards. I concentrated, forming more and more ice, *lengthening* the pillars, making me fly.

The breath ripped out of my lungs, and my heart slammed into my gut. I wanted to scream but couldn't gather enough air to do so. Rocketing through the air, wind tearing at my body, I began to fear I'd gone too far. The Ice exploded out of my hands, no longer creating the gentle crackling sound; it was more like an avalanche. Everything seemed out of control as the two pillars of ice shot me towards the helicopter in a mad rush.

It started to move forward, finally ready to leave. Kenji looked out, failing to hide his complete disbelief at seeing a boy catapulted through the air by shafts of ice. He quickly yelled something, and the chopper took off.

With a thought, The Ice changed direction, compensating for the movement of the helicopter, and I shot towards it, ice exploding in two streams behind me.

Within seconds, I was there.

Just as I was about to slam into the bottom landing leg of the helicopter, I exploded The Ice back into the air, releasing my arms.

The next seconds seemed to last a lifetime.

Knowing I only had one chance at this before I plummeted to the ground, I flailed my arms forward, trying to grab the left horizontal landing leg below the flying machine. The momentum of my flight slammed me into it, The Shield making the whole helicopter rebound violently. It wobbled and pitched, making me miss my chance.

I started to fall, the chopper five feet away.

I shot a stream of Ice towards the leg, freezing it solid. My fall stopped, my arm attached now to the chopper by a slender line of ice. The chopper flew forward, the sudden movement momentarily breaking my ice. It instantly reformed and started its fluid solidity that I had learned with the car chase. I swayed back and forth as the ice acted more like a rope than frozen water.

I tried something new, again.

With a thought, the ice between me and the leg of the helicopter began shrinking, slowly pulling me upwards. Mist from the releasing of Ice flew into my face, and soon I was only a foot or so underneath the leg. Wind tore at my clothes as the helicopter gained speed. It was difficult to breathe.

My hands touched the metal bar, and once I had a good grip, I released the remaining ice. I flung my legs upward and cradled the bar with my whole body, hanging underneath it. The helicopter was now ripping through the air at a petrifying speed. It also continued to gain altitude. I shot a glance below me. The ground was miles away, the freeway a ribbon of black against the green land surrounding it.

I looked back up, right into the eyes of Kenji.

He was not smiling.

✧❩✧❩✧

"You are a freak!" he yelled, the wind ripping his hair in all directions. "A monster!"

He pulled out a suitcase and hurled it at me, although he must have known it was useless. I sent waves of thought to The Shield, and the suitcase bounced violently right back at Kenji. He ducked inside, the bag narrowly missing him. It tumbled away, lost forever. Someone would need to buy new underwear.

I caught my breath, forcing myself to inhale and exhale, in and out, deeply. Then I let go of the metal bar with one hand, and shot a pillar of ice towards the top of the open side door. I froze it in a wide swath across the metal, then repeated the shrinking trick, letting go of the bar with my legs and other hand and shooting upward as the icy rope shrunk to only a foot, my whole body now filling the open doorway.

I swung my legs toward the inside of the helicopter, released The Ice, and slammed onto the floor of the cabin. Unbelievably, I had gone from the ground to a flying helicopter completely on my own. But there was no time to dwell on my new superhero powers.

I scrambled to my feet and got my bearings. Kenji was up by the pilot, leaning toward him and talking feverishly. My family members were tied and bound, each in a separate seat. The individual seats were spaced several feet from each other, forming a triangle. There were other empty seats surrounding them.

"Jimmy!" they all yelled at once as soon as I landed.

"Jimmy," Dad said, trying to be heard over the sounds of the rushing wind and beating blades of the helicopter, "How in the—"

He couldn't finish his question. Shock molded his features. Our family had been through a lot of crazy things, but they never expected to see me catch a flying helicopter.

I looked back at Kenji and the pilot.

With horror, I saw the pilot stand up, leaving the controls. He threw his helmet off, and he and Kenji slowly inched over to the other side of the chopper, to the open door directly across from me.

No one was left to man the controls.

The chopper continued to fly, but it tilted slightly forward.

"What are you doing?" I yelled. "I won't hurt you! Just land us and let us go. Please!"

"Sorry, little Fincher-san. I have no words to describe what you have *become*. But our battle with you, for now, is over."

Kenji looked at his comrade, and they turned their backs to me. My eyes had to be lying to me. They did not have parachutes attached to them. They couldn't possibly—

They did.

Together, the two of them jumped, pushing off with their legs as they dove forward into the mad wind. I ran across the cabin, screaming in disbelief. I gasped at what I saw.

Just before they left my field of vision, I saw the backs of their leather coats rip apart, and massive, black wings shot out behind them. Then, they were gone.

Something was wrong, something had changed. The black lance of shadow from the biker during our mad charge at each other, and now this. Raspy's little display back at The Pointing Finger. There was only one explanation.

The Shadow Ka were increasing their power, transforming their human hosts into something terrifying. The thought made me shiver, and I had to throw it out of my head. We had much bigger troubles, right here and now.

I whipped around and stared at my family.

Our time was short.

✧ ☽ ✧ ☽ ✧

The helicopter was now in a definite descent, the forward angle increasing by the second. Things started to slide from the back, odds and ends slamming into each other as they skittered toward the pilot chairs.

"Jimmy, hurry!" Dad yelled.

My mom was terrified, sobbing in fright. Rusty's eyes were full of panic, and he struggled against the ropes that bound him. I jumped into action.

I ran to the controls and looked around, desperate for an obvious sign of how to fly the thing. A huge lever sat in front of the main pilot chair, and I sat down to see what I could do. I pushed it forward, while kicking some pedal on the floor to my left, which was the worst thing I could possibly do.

With a horrible groan, the helicopter's front did a nosedive, and I flew out of the seat and slammed against the front windows. The Shield threw me back, and I reached out and grabbed the leg of an empty seat. The helicopter was now heading straight for the ground, and my family hung in their seats, facing downward, only in place because of the ropes that had been used to tie them there. Hanging from the seat, my legs pointed toward the front windows and the ground. I looked down.

The ground was coming fast, the ribbon that had been the freeway growing thicker by the second.

The Shield. The Shield was our only chance. I had to be touching each member of my family when we hit the ground.

I shot a beam of ice towards the very back of the chopper, then shrunk it, pulling myself up until I was hanging between Mom and Dad.

I frantically looked around. The seats were too far apart for a family hug. Another look down.

Rocketing towards the ground. We only had seconds.

I looked at Mom's ropes, and with a thought, froze them solid with ice, wishing them to be as brittle as possible. Not understanding, and not caring, Mom ripped her arms and legs free, shattering the frozen rope into a million pieces. She immediately fell.

I kicked my legs out and wrapped them around her middle, catching her, then froze her to my legs with ice to be safe.

I could feel the ground rushing towards us.

Another quick thought, and the sound of breaking ice came from above. Rusty immediately fell toward us. He slammed against me, and it took every bit of effort to maintain the icy hold I had to the back of the cabin. He wrapped his arms around my neck, squeezing the breath from me.

The ominous presence of the approaching ground made my heart skip a beat.

I looked down and reached for Dad with my free hand, looking through the windows on the front of the chopper. Time was out.

The blades of the chopper hit the ground, life seeming to transform into slow motion as I saw them bend. My hand found Dad's neck as the sound of crunching metal filled the air.

I pulled us to him with my last ounce of strength, and shattered his ropes with The Ice.

As flame and metal and glass exploded in a swarm of destruction all around us, I froze my family into place, with ice so powerful I knew our hug could not be broken.

Flames licked at us from all directions as the fuel from the helicopter exploded with a fiery roar. It never reached us. The Shield formed a perfect bubble of air, protecting us. We were encased in fire but felt no heat and suffered no wounds.

We slammed into the ground as one, The Shield bouncing us back towards the sky, sending us straight through the burning and exploding remains of the helicopter. We tore through the flame and metal, erupting into the open air with a rush of wind, clinging to each other in our icy grips. Mom's screams pierced the air as we fell back to the ground.

Fifty feet from the disaster, the ground rushed up at us until the outer edges of The Shield slammed into it, once again catapulting us into the air, although lower than the first time. The silence of Mom catching her breath only lasted a second before her shrieks once again boomed forth. We fell again, still clasped in our icy family hug.

Another bounce, another scream, another bounce.

And then it was over.

✧)✧)✧

I released the ice, and we fell off each other, our backs thudding to the ground. Panting, we stared at the sky above us, shock overwhelming disbelief.

It had been too close. More than ever before, it had been too close. Tears came, the horror of it all just too much to bear. Dad sat up and reached out, and soon we were all hugging again, this time out of love instead of protection.

"Jimmy," Dad said, still catching his breath, "I don't know what you've been up to, but my goodness, boy. Thank you. Thank you for saving our lives."

We hugged again, and the touch of family, reassuringly safe, brought my emotions under some semblance of control.

Dad got to his feet, and helped the rest of us do the same. As one, we looked back towards the burning wreck. The spectacular display of fire was not what made me gasp.

Standing between the inferno and us were people.

Normal, Japanese people. Forty or fifty of them. Everyday citizens.

Every face stared back, filled with uncertainty. Filled with wonder. Many were holding cameras or camcorders. I glanced toward the freeway and noticed cars were pulled to the side of the road. I looked back at our audience.

And then, it hit me.

It was no longer a secret.

Now, the world would know.

The world would know about me.

The world would know about Jimmy Fincher.

✦CHAPTER 40✦

The Guide

The thundering of hooves broke through the dumb-founded chatter of our onlookers.

Rayna, Tanaka, Hood, and Miyoko. Baka was there alongside them, and my heart lifted at the sight of him.

I had never seen the members of the Alliance so excited. They jumped from their horses, and took their turns giving me bear hugs and slapping me on the back. Tanaka used it as an excuse to hit me especially hard, and almost as if it were a joke, The Shield did nothing to stop him. He also made some smart aleck remark about how slow I was when I flew onto the helicopter with the pillars of Ice. So I took it on myself to wrestle him to the ground and rub his face in the dirt. The grime did nothing to our spirits—we laughed the whole time.

I introduced everyone to my family, and there were handshakes and hugs all around. Hood bent down and wrote something on the ground with his finger.

"FINCHER FAMILY, I AM HONORED. I AM YOUR SERVANT."

The whole scene was beginning to turn into a circus—gawkers with cameras, my family stunned from seeing a man paint with his finger, our horses trotting around in excitement. It was time to get out of there.

Urging my family to save their questions for later, we hoisted ourselves onto the horses. Rusty rode with me,

Mom with Miyoko, Dad with Tanaka. Hood and Rayna rode alone.

We rode off into the mountains, our horses too fast and the terrain too rough for anyone to follow. We rode for hours, until finally we felt safe and separate from the world.

For the next few days, we lived like mountain men. Dad, Tanaka, and Rayna hunted for food. We bathed in the river. We slept under the stars. But most of our time was filled with updating each other on what had happened since our separation during the train attack.

Mom, Dad, and Rusty had been taken to a dirty old warehouse, where they were held captive in a locked office. They had been fed and treated tolerably, the Bosu Zoku realizing that they were the only hope to get me sidetracked from my quest. The trip to the helicopter was part of a plan to take them to another place, far from Japan, to persuade me to leave and give up on my search for the Second Gift. It seemed they were getting desperate, and that encouraged all of us.

One misty morning, the wispy clouds draped the surrounding forests of the mountains and the air was crisp and clean and refreshing. I woke up before everyone else and went to sit and look out on the valley. It wasn't long before my gazing was interrupted by a sound behind me, and it turned out to be Rusty. I told him to pull up a piece of ground and have a seat, which sounded way too much like something Dad would say.

"Jimmy," Rusty said, "we really haven't had much chance to talk since the train thingy happened. How are you holding up?"

My brother was three years older than me, but we were best friends. For some reason, when he asked me that, everything came crashing down, and I couldn't hold back the tears. Realizing that whatever he might say would just come out sounding stupid, Rusty just put his arm around me, and we both looked off into the valley below. He soon joined me in the crying department.

For several minutes, no words were shared, but plenty of tears were shed. And somehow those moments with my brother made everything in the world right again.

✧🌙✧🌙✧

Later that morning, we held a council. Farmer had assured me he would send a guide, but we couldn't wait around for that. We needed a plan of action. Just as the morning sun began to burn away the dew and the mist, bringing a bright cheerfulness to the day, something happened.

Something unbelievable.

Dad started the council by recommending a trip back to America. Rayna agreed, but Tanaka and Miyoko did not, wondering why going there would be any better than searching for the Third Gift in Japan. They debated back and forth, discussing various issues that had surfaced from their experiences that would perhaps give us some clue as to where the next Gift could be. The whole time, Hood sat and brooded, still recovering from his ordeal at Raspy's hands. We had yet to hear of that story. I sat and listened to the different arguments, pretending to think deeply about them, but in reality wondering about the Gifts and trying to guess what the next two would be. Mom was ensuring that no one argued too hotly. Somewhere in the middle of all the discussion, Rusty burped and ignored the scowl from Mom.

It was half an hour or so into the conversation when the remarkable thing happened.

We heard the mixed sounds of static electricity and ripping paper.

✧❨✧❨✧

It was a sound so familiar, yet so unexpected.

In the air above us, a small ribbon of black appeared, a rent of black emptiness, and two hands suddenly reached through it, popping out of the blackness. The black area seemed to close around his hands, ensnaring them. There was another sound of ripping. The black surged again, briefly expanding from the hands hanging in midair. Just as quickly, the Ripping violently closed back in on itself, barely missing cutting the person in half who fell through onto the ground in front of us.

The person was a man. He stood, turning around to gaze into our startled eyes.

"Don't worry," he said. "The Black Curtain is still blocked. It took an army of five hundred to open it for just that long."

The man was bald, the man was tall, the man was skinny.

The man was Joseph.

✧❨✧❨✧

Ignoring the fact that our eyes had grown to the size of grapefruits, he ran up to me and gave me a massive hug, then held me back with his hands to get a look at me.

"Ah, Jimmy," he said to my disbelieving eyes. "Adequate words ain't been invented to express my joy at seeing your little whippersnapper face, although it saddens me a bit to see it without a Braves hat on top. I got a lot to tell you, boy."

Then he stepped back and addressed everyone.

"There is no time. I'll have to explain along the way. I know where the Third Gift is located. We've gotta hurry and find a ship."

"A ship?" I asked, still so shocked that it surprised me when words came out of my gaping mouth.

"Yes, yes! C'mon, I don't have time to explain." With that, Joseph took off towards the valley below. He must have missed the fact that we had horses.

He turned his head and yelled back at us as soon as he saw that we didn't show any sign of following.

"Giddyup people! The Tower of Three Days is failing, and we have to get to the bottom of the ocean before it collapses!"

Wondering if Joseph had gone batty—but realizing that a crazy Joseph was better than anything we had at the moment—we gathered our things, jumped on the horses, and followed him anyway.

We descended the winding trails through briar, bush, and tree into the valley below. I couldn't help but think how unlucky poor Joseph had been so far in this mess, and how good it was to have him back again.

Just as promised, our guide had come.

The journey for the Third Gift would soon begin.

✧Epilogue✧

In the days ahead, stories would fill the papers, videos and special reports would fill the news shows, rumors and gossip would reach everyone around the world via the Internet, all debating the images and rumors of a teenage boy and his feats of impossibility.

There would be the usual cries of hoax and fraud, but the evidence had been overwhelming, the witnesses numerous. A boy had flown with rockets of ice, men had taken to the air with black wings from a doomed helicopter, four people had burst forth from an inferno and bounced along the ground in a protective bubble of air. An entire gang of Bosu Zoku had been obliterated, with no remaining evidence but puddles of water.

The world and its perceptions would forever be changed.

As for my family and me, we would have to avoid that world as best we could. There would be no time to show stupid human tricks on late night television. We had far more serious things to take care of. For days after Joseph appeared, we traveled at night, staying in out-of-the-way motels, and had our food delivered. It had been a crazy week as we'd journeyed back to the town of Kushiro, on the coast, where ships and boats were available.

At the moment, I was staring at a world of blue, and my face was green.

✧ ☽ ✧ ☽ ✧

The shock of seeing Joseph had still not gone away. He had been so busy the last few days that we'd hardly spoken, other than short exchanges here and there that only left me with more questions.

Most of Joseph's time had been spent looking for a boat.

He'd meant what he said about the ocean, and we agreed to go along with his plan. He searched and searched, finally finding a large, hefty, sea-worthy yacht to take us on a long journey, with a captain and crew and everything. How in the world he paid for it was beyond any of us. He would only say that things were not what they appeared to be, and that the whole concept of money wasn't really an issue. It sure seemed to be an issue when he showed up one day with a trunk full of crisp, green cash.

He promised us over and over that he had not robbed a bank, but could not explain to us yet how he had gotten it.

"Just look at it as a gift from the Givers, and quit worrying your little heads about it," he had said.

The yacht was huge, nicely furnished, and scary. The thought of being on that big boat in the middle of the ocean gave me the shivers. Now as I stood and gazed upon the rolling waves of the ocean, barreling through the waters toward our destination, my fears were realized.

The ocean was so big. The sheer size of it was over-whelming, almost feeling like it was on top of us instead of below us. I was having a very difficult time getting used to it. Not to mention the up and down motion that turned me green and kept me near the railing when I was outside and near a bucket when I was inside.

We were quite the group. Dad, the patriarch. Mom, the mediator. Rusty, my best friend and brother. Tanaka with his gangly eyebrows. Rayna in her green leather. Miyoko with her strong smile. Hood with his Bender Ring. Our crew (who couldn't help but give our friends of the Alliance the strangest looks now and then). Hairless Joseph. And me, of course. All riding on an expensive yacht, sailing towards a place that only Joseph seemed to know about—although even that was sketchy.

He had purchased enough maps before we left to start his own store, and spent every waking moment studying them. The Givers had given him specific guidelines, so he was busy trying to figure out where this Tower was located. The only hint he would share with us is that the tower was supposed to defy time, and that it was always simultaneously three different days at the tower. Three separate days, at the same time. This, of course, made no sense to any of us.

Nothing Joseph had said since his return made much sense. However, we trusted him, and knew we would be enlightened at some point. Farmer had told me a guide would be sent, and I felt sure that Joseph was the one.

Before we left shore, we'd paid for a place to keep our horses, and we were promised that they would be well cared for. I almost broke down and cried when we had to say goodbye to them. Baka had become like a brother, as moronic as that sounds.

Rayna also sent a message to Geezer before we left, saying that he was to gather as many members of the Alliance as he could, and to wait for our return. From what I knew of Geezer, it seemed impossible that he could accomplish such a task. But Rayna looked at me intently when I voiced that opinion, and assured me that Geezer had never, not once, failed a mission he'd been entrusted with. I often tried to imagine what other sorts of people made up the Alliance. For some reason, different versions of Tanaka kept popping in my head, so I gave up.

So, once again, on that massive boat in the middle of the ocean, all was well for a short period. There was time to be together as a family, to enjoy one another's company. We would never again take for granted the simple wonder of being safe and united. I would've thought it impossible, but the love I had for my family was now even stronger. They meant everything to me.

And so it was that one morning, I stood at the railing on the edge of the boat, staring at the passing waters of the ocean, its dark blueness both comforting and foreboding. It reminded me of the black eyes of Kenji, and everything we'd been through went crashing through my head.

Thought through from beginning to end, it was tiring. But this was my new life. And that morning, perhaps truly for the first time, I accepted it. The future of the world rested with me.

I also thought about the many questions that were still unanswered.

The other two Gifts, the strange evolution of the Shadow Ka in our world, the huge monkey in the woods, the black, gooey face that Rayna was carried into by the flying Ka. The questions were endless.

The image of stone beds filled my head, and I thought of the lingering mystery of the Stompers.

Farmer had said they were not what they seem. Since I had no notion of what they were in the first place, this didn't really help me very much. But Farmer had been emphatic in saying that we must speak of them in the near future, that they were not like anything we could imagine.

And, that the biggest surprise of all was still to come.

Something was missing. In all of it, in all my thoughts, in all my experiences, something was missing, and I could not grasp it. But I could sense that someday, when the entire truth was revealed, one way or the other, it would blow us all away.

The yacht rolled, and my stomach finally gave up. With a good bend over the railing, I tried to give some pre-chewed food to the beasts of the ocean. However, a sudden burst of wind changed its course, followed by a familiar Japanese yell of disgust from an open window below me, and I couldn't help but laugh, at the same time realizing that I'd better run and hide. Tanaka was quick.

As I looked for the perfect hiding place, my brain reminded me that dark days lay ahead, and I wondered for the millionth time if it was all worth it. Ducking behind a huge wooden box piled with all kinds of boat supplies, I decided that it was. There was a renewed hope, and we were doing the right thing in taking that big boat to the middle of the ocean.

I wanted the Third Gift.

To be continued in...

Book Three of the
JIMMY FINCHER SAGA,

The Tower of Air

About the Author

James Dashner was born and raised in Georgia but now lives in Utah with his wife and three children. He is currently working on a new series. James loves to hear from his readers. You can email him at author@jamesdashner.com.

About the Illustrator

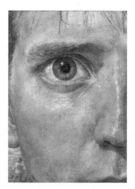

Michael Phipps grew up spending hours with friends drawing, imagining other worlds, making odd recordings, and building marble chutes and forts. He always knew he would be an artist as an adult, and he graduated with a bachelor of fine arts degree in illustration from the University of Utah. He loves to spend time with his family and friends, be outdoors, and listen to strange music. His art can be viewed at www.michaelphipps.net. E-mail him at art@michaelphipps.net.